HOW TO WOO THE WORLD'S FIRST VAMPIRE

3

LESSONS IN DIVINE DISASTERS

CARRIE PULKINEN

Lilith. She was the world's first woman. The Queen of the Night. The mother of all vampires.

She got credit for none of it, but after a few millennia of existence, praise…or even acknowledgment…for her contributions to society didn't matter. It all happened so long ago, and Lilith didn't hold a grudge against anyone.

Well, except for Adam, but that little weasel didn't count. He got her exiled from Eden, after all, and for what? Because she wanted to be on top for a change. Because she refused to *obey* him and wanted to be his equal. His partner.

Whatever.

Apparently, that was too much to ask because he'd kicked her to the curb and had her cursed to rely on the blood of mortals for sustenance. Of course, back then, Adam was the only mortal. Her curse was supposed to be a death sentence, but Lucifer had been kind enough to take her in. Demon blood had sustained her just fine…made her more powerful than those nitwits could have imagined. Now there were plenty of mortals topside to feast on.

Fuck you and the being who cursed me, Adam.

She groaned and pulled the blanket over her head. Why did she have to wake up thinking about *him?* Squeezing her eyes shut, she rolled to her side and willed herself to go back to sleep and have a pleasant dream for once. If only her magic worked on herself. She could glamour a heavy-weight boxer into eight hours of slumber, yet she couldn't sleep for shit.

It was time she dragged her butt out of bed and started her day…or night…whatever time it was. Lucifer controlled the "skies" in The Underworld, so who knew?

Percival called for his breakfast, and the gentle *caw, caw, caw* brought a smile to her lips. Lilith sat up, stretching her arms over her head, and her crow familiar flew from his perch to the bed before hopping across the deep blue comforter.

"Hello, moonlight. How are you today, my pet?" She stroked his sleek black feathers, and he answered with another *caw*.

"Okay, okay. I'll get up." She scooted to the edge of the mattress and placed her feet on the marbled concrete floor. Wiggling her toes, she focused on the smooth, cool surface, feeling the chill all the way to her spine. With a deep inhale, she stretched her arms over her head one last time before rising and padding to the pantry.

She filled his bowl with trail mix and gave him fresh water as he danced across the counter in anticipation. Dipping his head, Percival pecked at his meal, and Lilith strode to the terrarium, where Esther, her magical snake familiar, lay sleeping. Much like a chameleon, Esther could change her coloring to match her environment, her mood, or whatever the occasion might require. Most of the time, she took on the coloring of an overgrown scarlet king snake—red with black and yellow bands—a harmless, non-venomous creature. At four and a half feet long, she could be intimidating to some, but she was the sweetest, most adorable animal ever created.

Today, however, Esther had donned an albino white aesthetic. *That's new.* She'd coiled herself on top of a large, flat rock beneath the heat lamp, her face pointed toward the wall. Lilith stood in front of the terrarium and crossed her arms, waiting for the snake to lift her head.

"Good morning, love. It's time for breakfast." She tapped on the glass, but Esther refused to acknowledge her. "Come on, my little danger noodle. We have things to do. We have to…"

Lilith pressed her lips together and drummed her fingers against her biceps. What, exactly, did she have to do? Lucifer didn't require her to work, so she had no job. She had plenty of blood in the fridge, so she technically didn't need to go hunting—though, nothing beat a meal straight from the vein. Grabbing her phone from the nightstand, she opened the calendar app, and her shoulders slumped as she took in all the empty squares on the screen. Her schedule had been wide open for weeks. There wasn't a damn thing she had to do today.

"Maybe we can meet Eve for a drink."

Esther still didn't move, so Lilith used telepathy to send her thoughts to her familiar. *"Don't make me traipse through the streets of The Underworld without my favorite accessory."* Lilith was rarely seen without her snake draped over her shoulders. Percival traveled everywhere with her as well, but her crow preferred flying as his mode of transportation.

The snake started to lift her head, a minuscule movement that stilled as quickly as it had begun.

"I feel you, sister." If Percival didn't need to be fed, Lilith would've been in bed as well.

Her crow glided into the room and perched on the edge of the terrarium before leaning in and cawing at the snake. Esther's skin rippled as if she were going to move but thought better of it.

"Come here, nope rope. Stop playing." Lilith reached inside and slipped one hand beneath Esther's head, the other a foot down below her belly. Normally the snake would have coiled around her arm before slithering up to her shoulder. Now her body hung like a wet noodle.

"Esther?" A sense of dread tightened Lilith's chest, dragging her heart down into her stomach. "What's wrong, my sweet?"

She laid the snake on the bed and crouched in front of her, running her fingers over her head. *"Connect with me."* Focusing her magic into her familiar, Lilith tried to become one with the snake. Esther was an extension of Lilith, created by Lucifer himself to be her companion in the early years of her cursed existence. She should have been able to bond her consciousness to her familiar, seeing through Esther's eyes as if they were the same being.

Something was wrong. Okay, that was an understatement because, as Lilith reached into Esther's psyche, instead of the loving little snake she adored, all she found was a void. Emptiness as dark and cold as the rumors about Lilith's heart.

"Percival, what's wrong with her?"

The crow landed on the bed and gently pecked at Esther's back. Her muscles crawled in reaction, but she didn't lift her head. Pressure built in Lilith's eyes as she dragged in a breath. Esther had been her companion for millennia, and she'd never seen her behave this way. Sure, she got moody every now and then, but who didn't? This was something else entirely.

"Esther, please." She slipped her hand beneath the snake's head, and Esther finally opened her crimson eyes. "There's my girl." Lilith tried to smile, but the fear making her muscles tense wrapped around her heart, squeezing it until she thought it would burst like a tapioca pearl in bubble tea.

Esther's forked tongue darted out, lapping at Lilith's wrist before the snake closed her eyes and stilled.

"Oh, my baby. Let's get you back under your lamp." Lilith gathered her familiar into her arms and returned her to the terrarium before looking at Percival. "We need a doctor. Are there any vets in The Underworld?"

She tapped a finger against her lips. What exactly could a vet do for a magical snake? Esther was no ordinary serpent; she was an immortal, created by magic. Lucifer's magic. It was time she paid the ruler of The Underworld a visit.

Lilith sank into a blue velvet chair and folded her legs beneath her. Closing her eyes, she focused her magic on Percival and formed a connection with him instantly…the way it should have happened when she tried with Esther. Her consciousness melded with the bird's, and she stared back at herself through his eyes.

Her long red hair, which usually flowed in silky waves, was a matted mess, and her skin, which was always pale because she was a vampire, had taken on an ashen pallor. Whatever illness was affecting Esther appeared to be affecting her too. She shuddered at the sight of herself before taking control of her crow familiar and flapping his wings.

She soared out an open window, gliding over The Underworld toward Lucifer's palace. The Underworld used to be all fire and brimstone, which Lilith preferred—not that anyone asked her. Now it was a quaint little village with shops and cottages, and the ruler of The Underworld had done it all for Clara, his "soulmate."

Lilith blew a puff of air through Percival's nostrils. *What a crock.* Soulmates didn't exist, and she was undead proof. If they did, she'd still be head over heels for that alphahole, Adam, but she wouldn't touch him with a ten-foot stake…unless she could ram it through his chest.

Anyway… When Lucifer met Clara, he transformed The Underworld into what it was today so she'd be more comfortable, which wasn't surprising. The ruler of The Underworld had a soft heart beneath all those muscles and devilish good looks. He'd taken Lilith in, after all, given her a home and enough demon blood to keep her going until she could venture topside for the delicacy of humanity. And Esther… He'd given her Esther, and now he would heal her.

She arrived at Lucifer's palace and circled the medieval castle. Ivy climbed the silvery gray bricks, and three massive towers ascended into the sky. Finding an open window, she soared past the ruby red curtains and landed on a chandelier, cocking Percival's head and listening for sounds of movement.

A deep belly laugh echoed from the corridor to

her right, so she followed the noise and found Lucifer sitting at a table with Clara. Her long, white hair glistened in the lamplight, and whatever she'd said must've been hilarious because she had Lucifer in stitches. Lilith had never seen the man so...happy. *Must be nice.*

She landed on the table and squawked, and he finally got control of himself. With a deep inhale, he wiped a tear from his eye and took Clara's hand. He glanced around the room, leaning back in his chair to peer through the doorway.

"Hello, Lilith. To what do I owe the pleasure...I would say of your company, but it appears you've sent only your familiar."

"I need your help," she said into his mind before vocalizing, "Caw, caw!"

He rubbed his thumb and forefinger on his chin. "I see. Well, I am a busy man."

"You speak crow?" Chole gave him a quizzical look.

Lucifer chuckled. "Lilith is using telepathy. I hear her thoughts."

"Now that would be a cool power to have. Hi, Lilith."

"Hello. I'm sorry to interrupt, but I desperately need Lucifer's help."

"Indeed." Lucifer waved a hand at Percival like he was trying to shoo her familiar away. "Leave us, Lilith. Clara was in the middle of a hilarious story."

She narrowed the crow's eyes and pecked at his hand before letting out an ear-piercing *squawk*. *"Damn it, Luce, it's an emergency."*

Lucifer's eyes turned molten red, and if it were possible for steam to shoot out of his ears, it would have. In hindsight, pecking the ruler of The Underworld wasn't in her best interest. She'd known the man for eons, and his temper was like lightning. Thankfully, Clara stepped in.

She rested her hand on his shoulder, and his anger visibly simmered, the red in his eyes dimming as he covered Clara's hand with his. "Hear her out, honey. She flew all the way here."

"Anything for you, my love." He tugged Clara's hand to his lips and kissed her fingers before focusing on Lilith. "What seems to be the problem?"

"It's Esther. She's sick."

He laughed. "Nonsense. I created her."

"She's not moving. I barely got her to open her eyes this morning, and I can't connect with her."

His brow furrowed, his forehead pinching as if her words perplexed him.

"What's wrong?" Clara asked.

"She claims her reptilian familiar is ill."

Clara gasped. "Oh my. How can we help? Do you need me to call a vet? Do you need help getting her topside?"

Finally, someone was listening to her. *I don't think a vet can help. I need Lucifer to look at her.*

Clara smacked him on the arm. "You're not too busy to aide an ill animal, are you, dear?"

"No, my love. I suppose I'm not." Lucifer arched a brow at Lilith. "Give me five minutes to say good-bye, and I will be there."

"Thank you, oh great one." The sarcasm she tried to lace into her words didn't sound quite as good through the filter of Percival, but Lucifer smirked, so the message was received.

Lilith released control of her familiar—she'd be sure to give him extra raisins in his trail mix tonight—and returned her consciousness to her own body. Rising to her feet, she paced to the front door, though why she bothered, she wasn't sure. Lucifer appeared in her living room a minute later, bypassing the formality of knocking. Not that Lilith could complain. She'd done the same thing to him through Percival.

"Thank you for coming." She held his gaze, waiting to be berated for barging in on his quiet time with Clara, but Percival flew in through the window and perched on the back of the couch to caw at Lucifer.

"Percy." Lucifer ran the backs of his fingers over the crow's feathers. "I'm glad to see you've returned to your old self, my friend." He looked at Lilith. "Lead the way."

"She's in the bedroom." She strode down the hall and tossed her hair behind her shoulder, but her fingers caught in a tangle. She nearly ripped out a lock by the roots trying to free her hand, and she bit the inside of her cheek to keep from shouting profanities at the rat's nest she'd allowed her mane to become.

"How long has it been since you left your house?" Lucifer stopped in the doorway, crossing his arms and raking his gaze up and down her form.

She gaped at him like he was crazy. "I was just in your palace. I know you've only got eyes for Clara these days, but we had a conversation."

He shook his head, clicking his tongue like a disappointed father. "Percival was in my palace. How long has it been since *you* left your abode?"

She shrugged a shoulder and lifted Esther from her rock. "A while. Please, you have to help her." She shoved the snake into his arms.

Lucifer cradled her familiar, closing his eyes and stilling, focusing his magic into Esther. His mouth pinched, and he carried her back to the terrarium, returning her beneath the heat lamp and running a finger along her scales. "I can't help her."

She laughed, unbelieving. "What do you mean you can't? Of course you can. You're Lucifer Fucking Morningstar. You can do anything."

An amused grin lifted his lips. "Thank you for the ego boost, not that I needed it. I'm afraid, however, that Esther's condition is irreversible."

Her stomach dropped so hard she clenched her cheeks to keep it from falling out of her butt. "Irreversible? But she's immortal. Are you saying she's going to be a zombie snake for the rest of eternity?"

He lifted a finger. "It's irreversible unless…"

Lilith leaned toward him, her weight shifting so far forward she nearly toppled over. Straightening her spine, she parked her hands on her hips. "Would you care to elaborate, oh great one?"

"I created Esther to be an extension of you, the same for Percival."

"But I can't connect with Esther anymore. She's lethargic, and she's lost her color. What's wrong with her?"

"I rather hoped you'd figure it out on your own."

Lucifer sighed. "Tell me, Lilith. Have you looked in the mirror lately?"

"I saw myself through Percival's eyes before I sent him to your palace." What was he getting at? Her first and best friend lay lifeless—not in the acceptable, undead way—and Luce was asking about mirrors.

"And how do you think you look?"

Sweet Persephone, tell me he's not going there. A cramp seized her tightening jaw. "My appearance has nothing to do with Esther's condition."

"Doesn't it, though?"

"No, it doesn't. Do you hear yourself?" Leave it to a man to blame a dire situation on a woman's unkempt hair. *Typical.*

"You're not taking care of yourself, Lilith, and until you do, I'm afraid Esther will remain a 'zombie snake.'" He made air quotes before turning on his heel and striding out of the bedroom.

Lilith followed him down the hall. "I don't understand."

"She feels what you feel, and you, dear Queen of the Night, are a miserable, lonely wretch."

"How dare you?" She crossed her arms, and though she was tempted to stamp her foot, she refrained. Lilith was not miserable or lonely. She had plenty of friends. Hell, she was thinking about meeting Eve for drinks this afternoon. So what if she hadn't felt like leaving her house in the past week or three. She had enough blood in the fridge and pet food in the pantry. She had her books, TV, and her phone. It wasn't her fault the modern world made going outside utterly unnecessary.

"I call it as I see it." Lucifer gave her a sympathetic look. "You need help, Lil."

"I don't…" She scoffed. "If Esther were sick because of me, then Percival would be too. They're both connected to me."

"Indeed. If you continue your current path, your crow will be a sitting duck, and I'm afraid both their conditions will be terminal."

"Terminal?" Surely he didn't mean…

"They will not survive this, Lilith. If you want to help your familiars, you must help yourself."

"They'll die?" Her jaw trembled, so she clamped her mouth shut.

"Yes."

Her throat thickened. She was responsible for poor Esther's condition, and if she didn't fix it, she would die. How could she have let this happen? She loved her familiars more than anything in the world. Hell, they were the only creatures she'd ever loved.

"What can I do?" Her voice sounded tiny.

"Go to the counseling center and ask for Azrael. I'll let him know to be expecting you. I'm sure he can partner you with someone to help you work through your…issues." He curled his lip. "And Lilith, take a shower before you go. You stink."

CHAPTER TWO

Spencer Monroe eyed the hole in the side of the cliff. It couldn't have been more than two and a half feet in diameter—a tight squeeze in human form, and who knew what lay waiting inside. If he could shift into his owl, he'd have no trouble getting in. Sadly, a group of locals—all human— had gathered to watch.

"Cameraman always goes first." Alan clapped him on the shoulder. "You know how this works."

Yes, Spencer knew how shows like this worked. Though he'd only been part of *The Hunt for Cryptids* for a couple of months, he'd been a cameraman for a decade. And yes, he realized the irony of an owl shifter working for a show that was supposedly trying to expose the existence of supernatural beings.

Even more ironic? Every member of the team had some sort of magic, and the icing on the cryptid cake… The show's host, Alan Peterson, was Bigfoot himself. Of course, they'd never *actually* expose their kind. But humans ate this stuff up.

Spencer crouched in front of the hole and shined the light from his camera inside. Millions of tiny crystals encrusted the walls, reflecting the beam back at him. A bead of sweat rolled down his back, and he set the camera down to adjust his shirt. Living first in Arizona and then in L.A., he never understood the phrase "It's not the heat; it's the humidity," until he started traveling. The air seemed to wrap around him like a wet towel, never allowing his sweat to evaporate.

Summer in the rainforest was no joke.

He scooted toward the hole and rested his hands on the surface, peeking his head inside, and a woman from the crowd shouted in a native language. Spencer turned to see her raising her hands and closing her eyes as if she were praying. A very loud, *very* insistent prayer.

He looked at Juan, their local guide and resident alpaca shifter. "What's she saying?"

Juan fought his smile. "She says, 'The devil lives inside.'"

Spencer chuckled. Though he'd never been to The Underworld, he highly doubted the entrance to Lucifer's lair was a hole in the wall he'd have to lie on his belly to wiggle through. The devil seemed much more dignified than that.

"Be careful," Rebecca, a fox shifter and the second cameraperson said.

Spencer flashed her a reassuring grin. "Always."

"Get in there, man. We're burning daylight," Alan called before turning on his thousand-watt smile and narrating their adventure to Rebecca's camera.

Spencer worked his shoulders into the hole, inching the camera forward and army-crawling into the cave. Gravel clung to his forearms, and his pulse kicked into a sprint. Was he scared? Sure, a little, but that was part of the fun.

The tunnel opened into a small cavern. The crystals he'd glimpsed from outside lined all the walls and the ceiling, and another tunnel the size of a doorway stood at the opposite end of the space. Rebecca shoved a lamp through the entry, and he turned it on, illuminating the antechamber.

"You ready for me?" Alan's face appeared at the end of the tunnel.

"Yeah." A hissing sound reverberated through the cave. "No, wait." A three-foot-long snake slithered toward him, lifting its head, preparing to strike. "Shit! Viper!"

At the sight of the highly venomous reptile, Spencer's fight or flight instinct kicked in. Though, in his case, it was fight *and* flight. He called on his owl, and vibrating energy danced through his body. His skin pricked as feathers formed, his arms transforming into wings as he morphed into his bird. Flapping them, he took to the air a split second before the serpent struck.

Gods, I hate snakes. And for good reason. One of the nasty suckers had bitten him when he was a kid, and he'd spent a week in the hospital, nearly succumbing to the venom. Of course, that was before he learned to shift...and how to fight the little bastards.

"You got it, or do you need help in there?" Alan called.

Now, why would he ask a question like that? Spencer and Alan had been friends since middle school. He'd seen Spencer take on plenty of snakes. They weren't his bird's favorite food, but owls were opportunistic hunters. Plus, the only good snake was a dead snake. Anyway, Alan wasn't expecting an answer. All Spencer could do in his owl form was hoot.

He circled the cave once before swooping down and clutching the serpent in his talons. With a snap of his claws, he eliminated the threat before tossing it aside and returning to human form. He scanned the cave, checking the crevices for any more dangerous residents before picking up his camera and pointing it at the opening for Alan to make his grand entrance.

"It's taken care of. Come on in."

"According to locals…" Alan grunted as he worked his way through the hole. "This cave entrance was uncovered last year, and no one has dared to venture inside." He rose to his feet and dusted off his shirt. "Legend states that the devil lives here, and I'll be the first person to see the inside of his lair."

Alan winked, and Spencer rolled his eyes. As the host of the show, Alan always said things like that. He was "the first" to see so many things. Did anyone wonder how the camera got inside to record Alan being "the first?"

The cameraman took the initial risks, but he got none of the credit. Not on this show, not on his previous assignment, and Spencer was fine with that. This was his dream job. All the adventure, and no fans chasing him down for autographs when he was trying to have a nice dinner at a restaurant. He didn't want the limelight or the ego that came with it.

Rebecca followed Alan inside, and they filmed their search for the devil in the cave. Of course, they found nothing in the antechamber. The viper lying in wait was the most exciting thing so far.

"Damn, man. Couldn't you have subdued the snake and let me take care of it on camera? This adventure might not even make it on the air."

"I'm not a snake charmer. Why don't you head in first next time? We can get you a helmet cam."

Alan narrowed his eyes. "And risk getting mauled by a badger? No thanks. This face is my moneymaker."

Spencer laughed, but his friend was right. Women made up eighty-five percent of their viewership, and Alan's wavy blond hair, bright blue eyes, and chiseled features had a lot to do with it.

Spencer didn't mind badgers. The rush was worth it. "Ready to explore the rest of the cave, pretty boy?"

"You know it." Alan put on his television face, and Rebecca recorded him explaining more of the legend while Spencer ventured into the next chamber.

The main part of the cave stretched into the darkness, well past the light his camera emitted. He held up the lamp to get a better view and stepped farther inside, kicking up dust along the way. Scrunching his nose at the tickling sensation, he turned toward the entrance to film Alan stepping inside.

His friend's brown hat and serious expression made him look like Indiana Jones, which wasn't by mistake. Alan played the role of adventurous explorer to a T. Yet another reason Spencer would choose to be behind the camera rather than in front of it any day. He never had to put on a show.

Alan kicked up more dust as he moved, and the itchy sensation crawled from Spencer's nostrils down to his throat. He held up a finger to stop Alan's speech, but before he could hit pause on his camera, he let out a massive sneeze that echoed through the chamber, bouncing off the walls and reverberating through his chest. Pebbles rained down from the ceiling, and the entire cave seemed to rumble.

"That's not good." Alan backed toward the antechamber, and Spencer froze, staring at the ceiling as the falling pebbles grew into rocks the size of baseballs.

Now would have been a good time for his fight or flight to kick in, but he couldn't make himself move. A cracking noise echoed from above, sounding way too much like the ceiling splitting.

"Let's go, Spence," Alan yelled, snapping him out of his trance.

He started toward the antechamber, but the ceiling had, in fact, split, and as Alan darted through the opening, the baseball-sized rocks turned to bowling balls. The cavern roared as if Lucifer himself was pissed they'd ventured into his lair, and the ceiling caved right at the exit, trapping Spencer inside. Then there was silence.

Holding his breath, he waited for the dust to settle and his brain to grant him the ability to move again. He stood in the same position he'd frozen in, the camera still rolling, pointing at the rubble. Panning upward, he peered through the hole in the ceiling. Another chamber lay above, filled with even more glimmering crystals.

"Spencer!" Alan coughed, and Rebecca cried out, "Spencer, are you okay?"

"I'm fine." He kept his voice quiet to avoid disturbing what was left of the unstable cave ceiling.

"Spencer!" Alan called again.

He paced to the pile of rocks, gently placing each step, and lifted his head toward the small opening at the top of the passage. "I'm okay. Let me hand you the camera, and I'll fly out."

He gave the equipment to Rebecca, shifted into his owl, and passed over the mountain of rubble that would have sealed a normal person inside. The moment he returned to human form, Rebecca threw her arms around him. "Oh, thank the gods!"

"You scared the shit out of us, Spence." Alan wrapped an arm around his shoulders, giving him a brotherly squeeze.

"I don't think you have to worry about this adventure not making the cut." He picked up his camera and reviewed the footage.

"That's intense." Alan's eyes widened as he watched the video. "I knew hiring you was the right decision. After this, there's no way the network will cancel us. Screw Isabella. Our ratings are going to soar!"

Spencer ground his teeth at the mention of his ex-fiancée. Isabella DeFranco was the host of the most popular adventure show on live TV and every streaming service around. *Expedition Excitement* was huge, and so was Isabella's ego. Spencer had been her cameraman from the beginning…before the show took off and her self-importance skyrocketed. When he caught her cheating with the producer, he ended the relationship. In turn, Isabella ended his career.

"How will we explain Spencer's escape?" Rebecca asked. "There's not enough space above the rubble for a human to fit through."

Spencer eyed the ceiling. The antechamber

appeared stable enough. "Let's move some of the rocks. You can get a shot of Alan moving the last few, and then I'll pretend to come through. The editors can make it look believable."

"You're a genius. This is why we're best friends. I've got this. Back up." Alan shifted into his sasquatch, his body sprouting dark brown fur, his size more than doubling as his beast took control. He went to town on the rubble, lifting a three-foot boulder with ease. Five minutes later, his super-strength had enabled him to remove half the pile, and he returned to his human form.

Rebecca filmed the shots the editors would need, and they high-tailed it back to the hotel. That was enough excitement for one day. Spencer couldn't wait to get cleaned up and then stretch his wings beneath the moonlight.

After a hot shower, he wrapped a towel around his waist and found his phone ringing on the nightstand, Mandy's name lighting up the screen. He smiled and picked up the device. "Hey, sis. How's it going?"

"I'm good. How are you?" He could hear the smile in her voice.

"Oh, you know. Just working. Same old, same old."

She laughed. "Your job is never the same old anything. When will you be back?"

He glanced in the mirror on the dresser and tousled his damp hair. "We're heading home tomorrow."

"Perfect. You're going out with me Wednesday night."

"Oh?" He sank onto the edge of the bed. "Where to?"

"The Fang and Flask. We're going speed dating."

"The hell we are." He was still licking his wounds from Isabella's betrayal. He wasn't about to open himself up to dating anytime soon…if ever again.

"Please? Kathy was supposed to go with me, but she bailed. I really want to do this, and all my other friends are in relationships. Pretty please? For your favorite little sister?"

"Mandy…" He pinched the bridge of his nose. "I'm happy to hang out with you, but…"

"Fine. I'll go by myself. Hopefully there aren't any creeps attending. I'd hate to get abducted on my way home."

"You watch way too many crime shows."

"So do you, and you know what could happen to a pretty, young woman on the streets of L.A. all alone.

Especially at a place that caters to demons downstairs."

He closed his eyes, letting out a long sigh. "What time should I meet you?"

"Pick me up at seven."

"See you then." He mashed the End button and tossed the phone onto the nightstand. This was one adventure he was not looking forward to.

CHAPTER THREE

Lucifer was right. Not that Lilith stank. Aside from the whole drinking blood for survival thing, she was designed to be sheer perfection. Almost. Luce refused to give her wings when he took her in and made her irresistible to men, but otherwise, she could give Venus a run for her money in the looks and wiles department.

No, Lucifer was right about her becoming a miserable wretch.

She showered anyway—it had been a few days—and dressed in her favorite black catsuit. Esther still lay coiled beneath her heat lamp, and Lilith put a freeze-dried mouse in the terrarium before heading out the door. "Come, Percival."

Her crow flew after her, circling above her head as

she made her way through the village. She would never get used to The Underworld's new aesthetic, but if Lucifer could find happiness, so could she. Figuring out where the elusive emotion was hiding might be a problem, but Azrael could help her with that.

Holding her head high, she walked like a woman on a mission, her long strides carrying her down the street at a fast clip. The "sky" resembled daytime, with puffy white clouds dotting the fabricated blue background, and demons milled about, taking a break from whatever debauchery they should have been up to.

A beefy fiend with short black horns and fiery red eyes turned the corner and sauntered toward her on the sidewalk, walking right down the middle as if he owned the slab of concrete beneath his feet. He looked at her and continued his trek, fully expecting her to step aside like a good girl and let him pass.

"I am so not in the mood for playing chicken." She stopped and rested a hand on her hip.

The demon halted in front of her, holding out his hands in a *what the fuck are you doing?* gesture while simultaneously manspreading so she'd have to either step into the street or slither up the wall to move out of his way.

She didn't, of course, and instead offered a polite, "Excuse me."

"You're in my way," he snapped.

"And you're in mine."

"Remember your place, woman." His lip curled as if calling her a woman was supposed to be an insult. "You don't want to get kicked out of The Underworld too."

She threw her head back and laughed. These lower-level, testosterone-filled demons had no idea how tight she and Lucifer were. If this guy wanted to believe she was beneath him, she would have to teach him a lesson. "You'll be swimming in the tarpits before I'll ever be banished again."

He narrowed his eyes and growled, and she activated her glamour. His face fell slack as her trance took hold, and she used her magic to force him to his knees. "Having a pencil and a set of pinballs dangling between your legs doesn't make you superior."

She squeezed her fist, tightening her magic around his crotch. "I could render them useless with a flick of my wrist, so I suggest you remember *your* place."

"I'm sorry," he wheezed.

"Next time, don't be so rude." She released her hold, and he scrambled to his feet before darting around her and plowing down a witch in his path. *The nerve!*

The woman's butt smacked the pavement, and her coffee splattered on her lap as the demon booked it across the street without so much as an apology.

"I am so sorry." Lilith rushed to her side and helped her stand. "Are you okay?"

"My pants have seen better days, but I'm fine." She pulled a napkin from her purse and wiped the stain.

"I was trying to teach him not to be an ass to women, but my plan backfired." *Again.* It seemed like every time Lilith attempted to do good, she ended up making things worse for her effort. Perhaps she should simply stop trying.

"Some men will never learn, especially Barth." The witch shook her head. "He's a world-class asshole."

"Let me get you a new drink. It's the least I can do for causing you trouble."

"It's okay. I was about to toss it anyway." She threw the paper cup and napkin into a bin. "Thanks for standing up to him."

"Anytime."

The witch hung a left at the corner, and Lilith continued her journey. She entered the counseling center and strode straight to Azrael's office, where she found him sitting behind a massive black desk, his feathery onyx wings tucked neatly against his back. Pausing in the doorway, she tilted her head at the hot pink accents in the otherwise black space. As she stepped inside, the aesthetic morphed to match her favorite color—midnight blue.

"Since when does the Angel of Death like pink?" she asked.

He smiled wistfully. "Since he found his soulmate. What can I do for you, Lilith?"

Ugh. Not this soulmate business again. Ever since Luce supposedly found his, the entire Underworld had been buzzing about it. When would they all wake up and smell the O Positive? Soulmates weren't a thing, and they never would be. "Lucifer sent me. He said he'd call you."

Percival flew into the office and landed on her shoulder.

Azrael scowled. "So you're here by force. All the counseling in the world won't help someone who doesn't want help. I'm afraid you're wasting your time."

"I do want help. I need it. For Esther's sake." She strode to his desk and rested her fingers on the surface. "I need to talk to someone about my mood. Once they fix me, Esther will be healed."

"My team can't fix you. They can only listen and give advice on how to fix yourself." His gaze flicked to the doorway, and Lilith turned to find a vampire dressed in pink from her halter top to her stiletto boots. She carried two cups, one with a heart drawn on the paper sleeve. This must have been Azrael's so-called soulmate.

The woman's eyes widened, and she froze. "Sweet Lilith, it's you."

"Sweet. Now that's something I've never been called before."

"Sorry. I tend to take your name in vain more than I should. A lot of us do." She paced to Azrael's desk, kissed him on the cheek, and set down the cups. "I had a little fangirl moment there. I'm Deirdre." She offered her hand, and Lilith shook it.

"A pleasure."

"Oh, the pleasure is all mine. Believe me." She reached toward Percival, and the crow flapped his wings, cawing as he took to the air and landed on the back of the couch. "Sorry. Is that your familiar? Is it true you can put your consciousness in him, see through his eyes and stuff?"

"It is."

"Wow! I've heard rumors about your powers. I can glamour people, but that's as far as my magic goes. What else can you do?" Deirdre's smile was electric, and Lilith found herself returning the gesture. Though she was pale, as all vampires were, the woman seemed to glow with happiness. Her platinum hair was swept into a high ponytail, and her lipstick matched her outfit flawlessly. Deirdre would be the perfect person to get her out of this slump and have Esther feeling like her old self again.

Azrael cleared his throat. "I think Jessie might be a good match for you, Lilith. Let me pull up her schedule."

"I want Deirdre."

He blinked, a look of confusion flashing across his features briefly. "She's not a counselor."

Lilith brushed her hair behind her shoulder. "So? I like her energy. Do you have another vampire on your staff?"

"We're all dark angels."

"Well, Deirdre it is, then." She looked at her newfound friend. "When can we begin?"

Deirdre cut her gaze to Azrael before looking at Lilith. "I'm just a web designer. I'm not qualified to offer professional advice."

"Perhaps I don't need professional advice. Perhaps

I simply need a friend." She held up her hand, and Percival perched on her fingers.

Deirdre's smile widened. "You want to be my friend?"

"According to Lucifer, I'm a miserable wretch, and it's time I made a change. What do you say?"

"I say hell yeah!" She jumped, shaking her fists with excitement. "This is fangtastic! Want to go grab a drink at The Fang and Flask?"

"That sounds fabulous." She turned to Azrael. "Thank you for your help."

"Hold on." He raised a hand. "Lucifer said—"

"He said I needed to talk to you, which I've done."

The angel narrowed his eyes. "He said I needed to pair you with a counselor."

"And I've chosen Deirdre. Do not challenge my decision, reaper. You said yourself counseling doesn't work on the unwilling, and I am unwilling to talk to anyone but Dee." She looked at her friend. "May I call you Dee?"

"Of course." She rolled her eyes as if the answer were obvious.

Azrael let out a long, slow exhale and looked at Deirdre. "Let me know if I need to intervene."

Dee laughed. "We'll be fine. Ready?"

"I am." Lilith followed her out the door and glanced back inside the office. The moment she crossed the threshold, the deep blue accents returned to pink.

"Why does Lucifer say you're miserable?" Deirdre asked as they stepped onto the sidewalk outside the counseling center.

Percival perched on Lilith's shoulder, and she stroked a finger over his back. "I suppose it's because I am. I must be, or Esther wouldn't be sick."

"What's going on?"

"Nothing. I believe that's the problem."

Dee pursed her lips, and they walked in silence the rest of the way to the bar. Lilith chewed the inside of her cheek. Sharing the miserableness her existence had become would be harder than she thought. Her new friend idolized her, though she wasn't sure why. Everything Lilith touched turned to ruin: her marriage to Adam, her plan to rescue Eve, even the lesson she'd tried to teach the insufferable demon today had landed an innocent witch flat on her ass with coffee in her lap. Now she'd have to burst Dee's bubble and tell her just how lame the Queen of the Night had become.

They entered The Underworld portion of The Fang and Flask and made their way toward the bar in the back of the room. Tables dotted the center of the space, and a row of secluded booths lined the far wall.

"They have an amazing AB Negative on tap, though I guess you already know that," Deirdre said. "I'll get the drinks; you grab a table."

"Tell them to put it on my tab." Lilith chose one of the booths and slid onto a bench.

Dee returned with two goblets and sat across from her before taking a sip. "Mmm… If they didn't charge an arm and a fang, I'd give up hunting and drink this for the rest of my existence."

"It is a rare type." Lilith sipped the blood, closing her eyes for a moment as the warm, coppery liquid slid down her throat. "Where did you and Azrael meet?"

Her smile brightened her blue eyes. "Here, at speed dating, but we're supposed to be talking about you. What's wrong with your snake?"

Lilith ran her finger around the rim of her goblet. "She's an extension of me, as is Percival." She took the crow from her shoulder and set him on the table. "Their bodies can't handle my emotions. He'll fall ill as well if I can't get my act together, and…they both could die."

"He's beautiful." Dee reached toward him but

fisted her hand and jerked it into her lap. "He doesn't like to be touched?"

"Not by strangers, but I suppose that's an extension of me as well. I've grown rather…grumpy over the millennia."

She rested her elbows on the table and placed her chin on her hands. "Why?"

That was the million-dollar question, and though she hated to admit it, she knew the answer. Leaning back in her seat, she clicked her tongue. "I have no purpose."

Dee laughed. When Lilith simply arched a brow, her lashes flew high. "Wait. You're serious? You think you have no purpose? What about your job? What do you do?"

She lifted her hands before laying her palms on the table. "Lucifer took pity on me when I was cursed. After my work with the Adam and Eve apple debacle, he decided I'd contributed enough and has allowed me to stay in The Underworld rent-free."

Her new friend's mouth hung open. "When you say the 'apple debacle,' do you mean the whole serpent and the tree of knowledge bit? That was you?"

"It was Esther." She lifted a shoulder. "Well, it was me acting through Esther. I wasn't allowed back in the garden after my banishment, so I sent my familiar in my place."

"Wow." Dee shook her head in amazement. "Talk about getting even. You're the mother of retribution."

Lilith blew a hard breath through her nose, and Percival ruffled his feathers in response. "I wasn't trying to get even. I was trying to save Eve. After our creator lost control of me, I feared Eve wasn't shaped with the same free will. I simply wanted her to know she was her own person and didn't have to obey a man. Her giving Adam the apple wasn't part of the plan, but Lucifer was pleased with the mess I made of the situation."

She took another sip of blood and stroked Percival's wing. "Of course, Luce gets all the credit. Everyone thinks he shapeshifted into a snake, but it was Esther who sneaked into the garden. Hell, I don't even get credit for being the world's first woman most of the time. That title usually goes to Eve. It's like I've been swept under the rug."

Lilith tightened her lips, her jaw clenching. "Would you listen to me? I sound like a child. I don't need credit for those things, but I do need to find a new purpose for this existence."

"I give you credit. Those feats alone sound like a helluva purpose to me."

"A purpose I *had*. But what now?"

Deirdre chuckled. "Are you kidding? Lilith, you're the devil-damned mother of all vampires. You're the reason I am what I am. The reason I met Azrael. The reason thousands of us exist at all."

"I haven't turned anyone in centuries. I could cease to exist, and our species would continue to thrive. Vampires are doing just fine without me."

"You're still an icon, though. Hell, they named a whole music festival after you *because* you're the world's first woman."

Thanks to her refusal to obey Adam, she was occasionally used as the poster woman in the fight for equality, but… "Women have their own momentum. They don't need me."

Deirdre drummed her hot pink nails on the table. "I see where you're coming from. Your contributions to the world, while magnificent, happened long ago, and now you feel lost."

"Exactly."

She stilled her hand, tapping only her index finger. "You need a different mindset."

"And how do I achieve that?"

"Think of it this way. You've contributed more to the world than most ever will. Now, you're in retirement. It's time to start living your undead life for *you*."

Retirement. She'd never thought to look at her life in that way. Perhaps she didn't have to make another grand contribution to society. She could simply exist.

Her shoulders slumped. She'd been simply existing for the past who-knew-how-long, and look where that had gotten her. "I suppose I could get a job. Serving drinks here at The Fang and Flask could be nice. I'm sure Eve would hire me."

Dee shook her head. "Do something exciting. Take a vacation; go on an adventure."

"Perhaps I could learn a new trade. You said you're a web designer, right? Will you teach me? I could be your protégé. Tell me what it entails."

Deirdre screwed her mouth to the side. "I sit alone in my living room, staring at a computer screen all day."

Lilith curled her lip. "That sounds absolutely boring. No offense."

"None taken. I enjoy it, but I don't think it's what you need." She rapped a finger against her lips. "When's the last time you had a man in your bed? Or his bed, or the kitchen counter?"

Lilith tilted her head, biting her lower lip as she

tried to recall the last time she'd been intimate with anyone. "I don't remember."

Dee slapped her palm on the table. "There you go. You need to get laid, sister."

"It has been a while, but I don't believe sex will solve all my problems."

"It's a good start, though. Wednesday is speed dating night. You should come and find someone to hook up with. Who knows? Maybe you'll find your soulmate like I did." She wiggled her brows.

Lilith scoffed. "I have no soulmate."

"Everyone does."

"If I couldn't make it work with the man I was literally created for, I doubt, millennia later, someone will be created for me. I had my chance at love, and I chose freedom." Plus, the idea of one person being made for another—in a mutually compatible way—was total minotaur shit. Although, Lucifer had never been happier in his entire existence, and the bond between Azrael and Deirdre was palpable. Perhaps it was possible. Maybe…

Oh, get over yourself. You're cursed, Lil. There is no one out there for you.

"Okay, but you have needs, and I'm sure you can find a man to take care of them. Hell, you're drop-dead gorgeous. I bet you can snap your fingers, and they all come running."

She gave her head a tiny shake. Therein lay the problem. She could have any man she wanted, whenever she wanted. Well, the ones that didn't hate her for simply existing, anyway. Where was the fun in that? Her new friend was right, though. Lilith did have needs, and her vibrator wasn't bringing her the joy she thought it was.

Staying cooped up in her house for weeks at a time wasn't helping either.

"Or... Do you prefer women? That's a rumor that's been going around."

"I can see why people would think that, but no. I adore womankind. I want to be their friend, lift them up, and show them that they're queens, but I have no sexual or romantic interest in the female form."

"So you need a big ole dose of vitamin D. Sounds like speed dating is the answer to get things rolling for you."

Lilith sighed. "I've tried it before. There's far too much testosterone circulating in The Underworld. The entire bar will be filled with alpha males who either hate me for my confidence, want to conquer me for my strength, or both. Honestly, I wish I liked women. Dating would be so much easier."

Dee took a long drink from her goblet, her eyes calculating. "You need a cinnamon roll."

She furrowed her brow. "I prefer blood."

"Not to eat. Well…" Dee laughed. "I mean a cinnamon roll man. A sweetie pie. A nice guy."

"I'm more likely to find a hellcat that farts glitter and pukes rainbows. Nice guys simply don't exist down here."

"There's always the upstairs…" Deirdre sang as she lifted a finger toward the ceiling.

"You think I should hook up with a human?" Now there was an interesting concept. It had been ages since she'd communed with the living.

"You aren't looking for love, so why not? At the very least, you can make a nice meal out of him. If he's not a good match, you can glamour him when you're done so he doesn't remember a thing. Then you won't have to worry about him getting clingy."

She crossed her legs, shifting in her seat. "I don't know."

"I do. It's either this or you take a vacation. Nighttime skydiving could be fun. I'm happy to go with."

Adventure, excitement, sex. It sounded like the perfect recipe to turn her from miserable wretch to fun-loving creature of the night and save Esther in the process. She would start with the only one she was familiar with. "Okay, I'll do it. I'll go speed dating with the humans."

CHAPTER FOUR

"Lilith!" Eve shot to her feet, nearly knocking over her chair as she scurried around the speed dating registration table. Her pale pink dress matched the tablecloth perfectly, and her red stilettos clicked on the tile as she made her way toward her. "Where have you been? I was starting to worry about you." She air-kissed her on both cheeks before pulling her into a tight hug.

Percival landed on the table and pecked at the heart-shaped confetti covering the cloth.

Lilith pulled from Eve's embrace. "Percy, no! You know what non-food does to your digestive system. You'll be pooping paper for a week if you eat that."

The crow ruffled his feathers, picked up a paper

heart, and looked her in the eyes as he swallowed it anyway.

"Don't come crying to me when the constipation sets in, mister."

Eve crossed her arms and tapped her foot, looking at her expectantly.

Lilith gave her crow the stink eye before turning to her friend. "I've been home binging *Expedition Excitement*. I guess I lost track of the days."

"I haven't seen you in two weeks. I took your short answers to my texts as a hint you needed some alone time, but I was planning to knock down your door tomorrow if I didn't hear from you. What's going on? Where's Esther? I can't remember the last time I saw you without her."

Her mouth tightened. "Apparently, watching other people have fun on TV isn't the same as having it myself. Esther is sick because I've grown dull. Well…miserable if I'm being honest."

"Can't Lucifer heal her?"

"He said I have to heal myself, so here I am." She gestured to the room. "Ready for speed dating."

"If fun is what you're looking for, you've come to the right place." Eve took her by the shoulders and spun her toward the herd of beef corralled near the bar. "Look at the smorgasbord we have tonight. Yum."

Lilith let her gaze wander over the protruding muscles and gelled hair. Her nostrils flared as she inhaled the pheromones of a dozen alpha males, mostly demons, a few she'd already sampled. *No, thank you.*

One such demon, with hollow black eyes and an eight-pack hidden beneath his blue t-shirt, raked his gaze down Lilith's tight, black leather pants. She wore a matching halter top with silver snaps for easy release—her goal tonight was sex, after all—and her long red hair flowed in thick—untangled—waves over her shoulders.

His eyes locked with hers for half a second, and they turned to saucers in an *oh shit* expression before he jerked his head down and turned away from her. Lilith smiled. The demon—she couldn't recall his name—had been intent on conquering her. He'd been rough, believing he could put her where he wanted her and have his way with no regard for her pleasure.

He knew who she was, so why he thought he could dominate her, she wasn't sure. Well, that wasn't true. She did know. Testosterone. They were all the same. They all wanted to be the man who could tame the world's first woman. The one Adam couldn't control.

But it never failed. By the time Lilith was done with them, they'd be curled in the fetal position, practically sucking their thumbs. She didn't even have to use her glamour to have them falling at her feet.

Lilith's smile turned sinister. Maybe she should stay downstairs and show one of these meatheads what happened when they messed with the wrong woman. Putting assholes in their place always brought her joy in the past.

Eve rested a hand on her shoulder. "Do any of them pique your interest?"

If she was going to introduce change into her life, she shouldn't go back to her old ways. She wanted to experience this mysterious cinnamon roll Deirdre spoke of. "I think I'm going to try my hand upstairs tonight."

Eve blinked three times. "With the humans?"

"I'm on the hunt for a nice guy."

Her friend laughed. "Oh, wait. You're serious?"

"I am." She held out her hand, and Percival flew to her, perching on her fingers.

"If that's the case, you might want to tone down your…Lilithness. You can be intimidating."

Her lips parted on a theatrical gasp. "I can be nice as well."

Eve held in another laugh. "Be gentle with whomever you choose. We need the men to keep showing up."

"I'll be an angel." She winked and made her way past the beefcakes, through the purple velvet curtains, and up the stairs to the mortal realm.

Before she could step into the human half of the bar, Percival let out an irritated *caw*.

"I told you not to eat the paper."

He ruffled his feathers, giving his body a shake.

"I'm sorry, my pet. You'll have to make yourself scarce for a bit. Animals aren't allowed upstairs." He cawed again as she stroked his feathers, and she smiled. "Okay, behind the counter, and you stay there until I tell you otherwise. Fly low." She dropped her hand, and her crow glided along the floor before disappearing behind the counter.

Katie, the barista, gasped, pressing her hand to her chest. Lilith strode to the bar and lowered her voice. "Take care of Percival for me? I'm playing with the humans tonight."

"Lilith, sure." She scanned the ground, leaning to her left to see past the counter. "Should I be expecting a snake to slither in too?"

Lilith's lips tightened at the mention of Esther. She needed to remember the real reason she was here. To find happiness. Or to have a good time for a few hours at the very least. Poor Esther's health depended on it.

"It's just Percival tonight. I love the color of your hair, by the way. The golden-brown compliments your eyes and skin tone perfectly."

Katie ran a hand through her chin-length bob. "Really? It's a box job. I can't afford to have it professionally dyed."

"You don't need to. It's gorgeous."

A blush spread across her cheeks. "Thanks. Can Percival have a snack?"

"He would love one."

"What should I feed him?"

"He's a crow. He'll eat anything." Lilith turned and strode to the registration table, a six-foot foldable, draped in a deep red cloth. Pink heart confetti covered the surface, and behind the table sat none other than Venus herself.

The Goddess of Love and resident succubus tilted her head as Lilith approached. "You are the last person I'd expect to see up here tonight."

"I'm on a mission, and this is the best place to accomplish it." She closed her eyes for a long blink and inhaled deeply, focusing on the vibration of the room. The slight tingle of Venus's magic ran across her skin, making her arm hairs stand on end. "Giving the hu…the *people* a boost in the love department tonight, I see." She signed her name on the registration list.

Venus lifted a shoulder. "I feed off the matches made. It's just a little magic to ensure some happen."

"I don't need any help." Whatever happened tonight…whether she found a match or she simply spent some time talking to the living…she wanted it to be authentic. No help from the Goddess of Love required.

"I don't doubt that."

Lilith picked up a date card and a pencil. "What table am I at?"

"We're doing things differently tonight. The women are rotating." She tapped the phone lying on the table to check the time. "Let's get this party started."

Lilith joined the group of women standing at the front of the room while Venus grabbed a microphone and addressed the crowd. "Gentlemen, please take your assigned seats. Ladies, you'll have five minutes with each man. At the sound of the buzzer, you'll move on to the next one. Feel free to take notes, exchange numbers, hook up after we're done…whatever you want to do. But most of all, have fun!"

The first buzzer sounded, and the women filed into the speed dating zone, with two rows of tables, a man at each one. Lilith stood in the aisle between them, scoping out her potential victims…er…dates.

Venus clutched her arm, steering her toward a table. "Grab a seat. We're one lady short tonight."

Two chairs stood vacant. Across from one sat a hefty human with a buzzcut and biceps the size of barrels. He raked his gaze down her body, lingering on her chest and making Lilith's skin crawl. She took the chair at the table next to him, saving that unsavory experience for last. The poor guy might be in tears by the time she was done, and she didn't want to ruin his chance with the rest of the women. Some ladies went for the strong, dumb type. Far be it from her to judge.

"Hi." Potential victim number one forced a smile. He pushed his glasses up his nose and wiped a bead of sweat from his temple. "I'm Theo."

She folded her arms on the table. "You seem nervous, Theo. Why?"

He let out a dry chuckle and lowered his gaze. "I, uh…didn't expect all the women to be so beautiful."

She tilted her head. "Do beautiful women scare you?"

"Not normally, but I was hoping to make a match tonight. Everyone here is out of my league."

"Nonsense." She waved off his statement. "Everyone here is on equal footing, also looking to find a match. What do you do for a living?"

"I'm a computer programmer."

"And what do you do for fun?"

"I play video games, and I…" He laughed shyly again. "I like salsa dancing."

That could be exciting. Lilith hadn't been dancing in decades, but this guy's lack of self-confidence didn't do much for her in the attraction department. She was all about equality; she didn't want to dominate a man any more than she wanted one to dominate her. "Lead with that, and have more faith in yourself. There's someone for everyone."

Of course, she didn't believe that last bit for a second, but a little white lie never hurt anyone. The buzzer sounded, and she rose to her feet.

"Do you want to talk later?" Theo asked.

He'd finally dug up some courage, and he seemed like a sweet guy. A cinnamon roll, like Deirdre described, but his center was a bit too mushy for her taste. "Maybe I'll circle back. Have fun."

She moved to the next table, and then the next. Half the men she talked to rivaled the demons downstairs in assholery, but some of them were nice. Her chances of finding a man to light a fire in her core were better up here, but so far, no one had even created a spark.

She went through two more dates before her gaze landed on *him*. The man two tables down had light brown hair, sheared short on the sides and the kind of messy on top that could have taken him twenty minutes to mold into place or could have been the result of him running a hand through his damp locks and walking out the door. It didn't matter which; the style suited him.

He had kind eyes, dark brown in color, but the most intriguing thing about him was his aura. Magic sparkled around him, though what kind, she couldn't be sure. He didn't look like a demon, so he must be a topside being. Not a vampire; she'd recognize one of her own immediately.

She barely paid attention to the man at the table next to him, and when the buzzer sounded, signaling her turn to talk to the most intriguing person in the room, she shot to her feet and sank into the chair in front of him at vampire speed.

Venus cleared her throat from across the room,

and Lilith sent an *I'm sorry* to her mind. She'd already let her guard down, and she hadn't even spoken to the man yet.

They locked eyes, and an electrical sensation buzzed in her belly before zapping her chest. The man furrowed his brow, giving his head a little shake and straightening his spine. "Hi, I'm Spencer."

"Lilith." She offered her hand. "Pleasure to meet you."

He hesitated, eyeing her fingers like they might electrocute him if he touched her. Thankfully, he didn't leave her hanging, but when his palm touched hers, another jolt of electricity zapped her chest. He must've felt it too, because when he released her, he rubbed his hand on his jeans.

"Why are you up here and not down below?" she asked, lowering her voice so the humans wouldn't hear. "Most supes do their speed dating downstairs."

He cut his gaze from side to side. "I'm not here to find a date. I'm supporting my sister."

"Then why are you participating? The game is short one woman. If you stepped out, things would be even."

"It's hard to say no to Venus."

Lilith suppressed a grin. "Indeed, it is." Venus had an uncanny ability to predict matches. Whether they were love or sex matches didn't matter much; she could get her sustenance off either. If she insisted Spencer play the game, she had a reason, and hopefully, that reason was Lilith.

"It won't hurt to get to know each other in our five minutes, will it?" She lowered her voice again. "What kind of supe are you?"

He leaned toward her. "I'm an owl shifter."

Her brow shot up, and her heart thumped against her chest. "You're nocturnal."

"So are you." A sexy grin tugged at one corner of his mouth, making her stomach flutter.

"Look at that. We already have something in common."

He chuckled. "I guess we do."

"What do you do for a living?"

"I'm a cameraman for an adventure show."

She sucked in a breath. Now, there was a fascinating career choice. "Which one? Is it *Expedition Excitement*? I love that show."

"No." His eyes darkened briefly, like a storm rolling through that clears just before it can cause a flood. "I'm on *The Hunt for Cryptids*."

Lilith laughed. "A shifter hunting for cryptids? You can't be serious."

"Who better to put on a show trying to expose us than a group of cryptids ourselves?"

"A group? You mean you're all…?"

"Every one of us. Have you seen the show?"

"No, I assumed it was a bunch of humans being idiots. Now that I know, I'll be watching it for sure. Do you ever get any time in front of the camera?"

His cheek twitched as he shook his head. "Occasionally, but I prefer to be behind the lens. The limelight isn't my thing. What about you? I assume you're here to spice up your hunting routine. Looking for a meal or a date?"

"Both, actually. My life isn't nearly as exciting as yours."

He scoffed. "A virtually indestructible creature of the night with mind control powers? How could your life *not* be exciting? You can do anything you want."

"Well, I…" She clamped her mouth shut. How to tell the first man who'd piqued her interest in eons that Lilith, the mother of all vampires, had turned into a boring homebody?

The buzzer sounded, but lucky for her, the seat next to her was empty. She could spend another five minutes with Spencer before she had to move. "Sometimes, when you can do anything you want, nothing sounds appealing. But what you do…tell me more. I'm intrigued."

As he held her gaze, her stomach flip-flopped and something akin to excitement flowed through her veins. She would have to thank Deirdre for insisting she come here. This was exactly what she needed.

He shifted forward, leaning a forearm on the table. "Alan Peterson, the show host, is a sasquatch."

She giggled like a schoolgirl. "Really? Do you ever hunt for Bigfoot?"

"All the time. We go all over the world, investigating claims of the supernatural. Of course, we never expose anyone, but the humans don't care that we never find anything. Or…they used to not care."

She tilted her head, silently urging him to continue.

"The network is threatening to cancel us if we don't make the show more exciting. They want us to find more evidence, but how can we? The world isn't ready to know about us all." He blinked, his lips puckering like he couldn't believe he'd told her that.

"What are you going to do?"

"We experienced a cave-in a few days ago in the rainforest. We got it all on film, so hopefully, that will appease the network gods for now. If not, I don't know."

He told her more about the program, but the damn buzzer went off again. The woman next to her stood, ready to meet Spencer, but Lilith wasn't done with him yet. She activated her glamour, encircling Spencer and herself in a bubble of invisibility.

The woman's expression pinched, but then it smoothed as she walked past them and sat at the next table.

Spencer arched a brow. "What was that?"

"I'm enjoying myself, so I used a little magic to hide us."

"Isn't that cheating?" He scooted his chair forward, tucking himself into their date.

She leaned an elbow on the table and rested her chin on her fist. "You're only here to support your sister. It's better not to get anyone's hopes up, don't you think?"

His gaze never strayed from her eyes. "I suppose."

"Why didn't your sister bring someone who wanted to participate?"

"She was supposed to come with a friend, but she canceled. Mandy didn't want to come alone, so here I am."

"That's very sweet of you." Cinnamony sweet.

"What can I say? I'm a nice guy." He cleared his throat. "You haven't told me much about you."

Eve's words echoed in her head: *Tone down your Lilithness; you can be intimidating.* Apparently, a woman not putting up with a man's shit made her threatening, and her reputation of zero bullshit tolerance preceded her. Spencer either hadn't made the connection that she was *the* Lilith, or he was giving her a chance to prove herself. She hoped it was the latter. It would be nice if someone would get to know her before judging her for getting kicked out of Eden. She was enjoying his company too much to risk it being the former. The less of her "Lilithness" he learned about now, the better.

She turned to gaze over her shoulder. "Which one is your sister?"

He nodded toward a woman a few tables away. "The blonde in the white shirt."

"She's pretty." Lilith blinked, unable to detect a hint of magic in her aura. "Is she human?"

"Yeah. Her dad's human; mine's the shifter."

"Fascinating." She turned toward him. "Does she know about our kind?"

He nodded slowly. "Kinda hard not to when your brother turns into an owl for the first time at the dinner table, wings flapping in the mashed potatoes because he's not sure how to use them yet."

She laughed. "Oh, I bet that was a hoot."

He chuckled. "Yeah. A real *hoot*, for sure."

"Oh." Lilith pressed her fingertips to her lips. "I wasn't trying to poke fun."

"It's all right." Heat sparked in his eyes, and for the first time since she sat down, his gaze wandered down her form. When he reached her eyes again, her chest burned in a most pleasant way. "What about you? How'd you become a vampire?"

A buzzer sounded before she could answer, signaling the end of speed dating. The people around them began to stand, searching out the ones they'd felt a connection with, but Lilith and Spencer remained in their seats.

With his palm flat on the table, he tapped his index finger on the cloth. "Are you free tomorrow?"

She was hoping for some action tonight, but Spencer seemed like a man worth waiting for. "I am."

He cast his gaze over her shoulder. "Can you unglamour us? My sister is looking for me."

"Of course." Lilith reined in her magic, and Mandy approached, confusion drawing her brows together.

"Where have you been, Spence? I thought you decided to speed date, but I never sat with you."

Spencer winked at Lilith before rising to his feet. "A vampire held me hostage. Mandy, this is Lilith."

Lilith stood and shook Mandy's hand. "Thank you for dragging him out tonight. I've had a wonderful time getting to know him."

Mandy cut her gaze between them before grinning. "I'm glad someone made a match. I didn't click with anyone."

"I'm sorry to hear that," Venus said as she approached. "I do hope you'll try again next week. I'll do my best to find someone for you."

Mandy shrugged. "Thanks. I might."

"And you." Venus wrapped an arm around Lilith's shoulders. "You found the only other magical being in the room. I knew there was a reason he had to participate."

An adorable blush rose on Spencer's cheeks, and Lilith's pulse quickened again.

"Don't let the rumors fool you." Venus took Spencer's hand, holding it between both of hers. "Lilith isn't the demon people make her out to be. She was kicked out of Eden for wanting equality. Nothing more. Remember that."

Spencer's face fell, and he slipped from Venus's grasp. "I didn't realize you were… You're *Lilith*."

Her heart sank into her stomach. She had her answer. He was only friendly with her because he didn't know. Cue the testosterone overload. If her previous experience with men—and she'd had millennia of it—was any indication, his sweet demeanor was about to shift to asshole mode. "Yes, I'm Lilith."

"We should go, Mandy." Spencer jerked his head toward the exit.

"Umm…" Mandy looked from him to Lilith. "Okay?"

Lilith crossed her arms. "What about tomorrow? Weren't we making plans?"

Spencer's jaw tightened. "I'm leaving for Costa Rica the next day, and I need to pack. It was nice to meet you." He nodded once, turned on his heel, and strode out the door.

Venus's jaw dropped. "What in Lucifer's name just happened?"

"He's a typical man." Lilith inclined her chin, hoping it would ease the sting of rejection. It didn't. "Once they find out who I am, they either want to conquer me or want nothing to do with me."

"Pfft." Venus waved a hand dismissively. "Have you ever met a man you couldn't seduce?"

"Of course not." But she wasn't trying to seduce Spencer. She'd let her guard down and had actually started to like him. What was wrong with her?

"Something is off about this. I'm never wrong when I make a match."

"It's fine. I should've stuck with the downstairs guys. At least they're not afraid of me." She turned to the bar to retrieve Percival and go home to lick her wounds. She'd have to find another way to save her snake.

"No, Lilith." Venus clutched her arm. "You don't understand. Spencer is your soulmate."

She laughed dryly. "There is no such thing."

CHAPTER FIVE

"What the hell was that?" Mandy grabbed Spencer's arm the moment they stepped onto the sidewalk. "I haven't seen you smile like that in ages, and you run off for what? Because she's immortal? Famous? Too beautiful?"

"All of the above." He shoved his hands into his pockets and paced toward the parking lot. *Don't let the rumors fool you.* He didn't have to. He'd let the woman do it on her own.

Mandy stood outside the car, peering at him over the top as he opened his door. He slid into the driver's seat and started the engine, and his sister slowly sank in next to him. Her jaw was tight and her nostrils flared as she stared out the front window, no doubt writing a lecture in her mind.

He was an idiot. He could see the power sparking in Lilith's aura, could sense she was a formidable being the moment she sat at his table, yet he'd allowed himself to be drawn in, to let down his guard, and to enjoy the attention of a beautiful woman.

Damn, she was good. Her feigned interest in his job and family had sucked him into her trap like a mosquito to a bug zapper.

Mandy puckered her lips, making a popping sound before she spoke. "She seemed like a nice woman."

"She's *Lilith*. She can't be nice." He pulled onto the street and headed for his sister's apartment.

"Then why did you talk to her for so long? Did she glamour you? Were you really held hostage?"

"She didn't glamour me. She used her magic to make us invisible so she wouldn't have to rotate, and I didn't protest. But that's her game, isn't it? Using her wiles to seduce men and drain their energy."

"She's a vampire, not a succubus."

His shoulders tightened, drawing toward his ears. "The world's first vampire. Who knows what kind of influence she has? I'm not about to get involved with a woman who has the power to ruin my life. Been there, done that, still paying for the t-shirt."

She narrowed her eyes at him before looking out

the windshield. "Whatever you say, big brother. I'd hate for you to give away your power. Though it sounds like Isabella still has control of it."

His teeth clicked as his jaw tightened. "She does not." His ex could choke on a pellet for all he cared. "It doesn't matter anyway. I'm leaving in two days. It's not like I have time to date."

"It sounded like you were making plans for tomorrow. I think you liked her and it scared you."

His slow exhale warmed the back of his throat as he stopped at the curb in front of her building. "Good night, Mandy."

"At the very least, you should apologize for leaving like that. It was rude. Mom raised you better." She climbed out of the car and slammed the door before he could respond.

It was just as well. His sister had a point. He *did* like Lilith, and it *definitely* scared him. He put it in drive and headed to his apartment. Dating had been the last thing on his mind since Isabella broke his heart and ruined his career. The moment Alan hired him onto the show, he'd buried himself in his work. Hell, he was probably driving their producer crazy with all the extra hours he was putting in "helping" the video editors.

He parked in the garage and mashed the elevator

button for the tenth floor before leaning against the wall and closing his eyes. *Damnit, Mandy, I see what you did.* Her friend hadn't canceled on her. She'd planned to take Spencer to speed dating from the beginning. He should have known.

And Lilith… Gods, she was beautiful. Smart and funny too. He couldn't remember the last time a woman had shown that much interest in him. Usually, as soon as they found out he worked on a television show, their questions turned to whether or not he could get them into parties, arrange auditions —as if he was a fucking agent—or help them meet the stars.

Lilith was more interested in what he did on the show than what he could do for her. She seemed genuinely interested in *him.* And that spark he felt when their eyes met? The electric jolt that zapped his heart when he shook her hand? It was enough to make his owl take notice, and that was the most terrifying part of all.

He'd made it a rule to never date vampires. The last thing he needed was to fall in love with an immortal being when he was going to grow old and die. Owl shifters had the same lifespan as humans, and he was already thirty-eight years down.

The elevator door slid open, and cool air wafted in from the hallway. He hung a left and paced to his apartment, his heart sinking lower with each step. Inside, he tossed his keys in the bowl by the door and grabbed a beer from the fridge.

Mandy was right, damn her. Spencer had been rude. Despite her reputation, Lilith had been nothing short of pleasant to him. He dropped onto the couch and took a long pull from the bottle. The cool, bitter liquid slid down his throat and churned in his stomach along with his guilt.

Though she'd held her head high as his demeanor had done an about-face, she hadn't hidden the disappointment in her eyes. They had a connection; there was no denying it. He'd let himself get swept up in the magnetic energy dancing between them, and he'd forgotten his *no vampires* rule. He'd forgotten himself.

His quick exit had been for his own benefit, and he'd disregarded her feelings. He'd been an ass, and he owed her an apology.

Lying on her side, Lilith held the pillow against her head, trying to drown out the incessant pounding noise. It had been two days since the speed dating incident, and the stupid seed Venus planted in her mind had already grown into a sapling.

Could Spencer be her soulmate?

No, the idea was preposterous. A soulmate—if they even existed—would never run out on the person fate chose for him. Not like that, with no explanation. Of course, he hadn't needed to explain anything. His facial expression alone had sent the message loud and clear.

Percival flew into the room and landed on her hip, pecking at her arm. *Caw, caw.*

"Leave me alone. Can't you see I'm wallowing in self-pity?"

He hopped onto her shoulder and pecked at her hand, which was holding the pillow against the side of her head.

"Percival, please." She tossed the pillow aside, and the pounding intensified.

"Lilith, I know you're in there," Eve's voice drifted in through the windowpane. "Either let me in, or I'm going to bust down your door."

She groaned and rolled out of bed. "I'm coming."

Poor Esther hadn't moved since the last time Lilith returned her to her terrarium, and she stopped, resting her hands on the cool glass as she gazed at her companion. "I'm sorry I failed you."

"Lilith!" Eve shrieked from outside the front door.

"No one has any patience these days." She paced to the living room and opened the door.

Eve and Deirdre stood on the stoop. Concern tightened Deirdre's eyes, but Eve parked her hands on her hips and shook her head. "It's about damn time." Without waiting for an invitation, she marched inside, and Deirdre followed.

"What in Lucifer's realm is going on with you?" Eve sank onto the sofa and crossed her legs. "We haven't heard from you in two days."

"We were worried." Deirdre sat next to Eve.

Lilith curled into the dark blue accent chair, folding her legs beneath her. "It's Venus's fault. If she hadn't coerced him into playing, I…"

"By him, do you mean Spencer?" Deirdre asked.

"Of course she means Spencer." Eve squared her gaze on Lilith. "Venus told us everything. You met your soulmate."

Lilith scoffed. "That's what she told you, is it? As if that could happen."

Deirdre folded her hands in her lap. "How's Esther. Has she shown any signs of improvement?"

"She ate the mouse I left for her while I was playing that horrid game, but by the time I got home, she'd returned to her rock and still refuses to move. I don't think having a little fun every now and then is going to save her. I need to do something else."

Eve screwed her mouth over to one side. "Do you—"

"What about The Fang and Flask?" Lilith asked. "I could work behind the bar, mixing drinks."

Wariness flickered in her eyes, and she fought a lip curl. "Umm… We're not hiring."

"Really? You seemed short-staffed when I was there."

Eve leaned forward to pat her knee. "No offense, hon, but do you remember what happened when you filled in for someone a while back? We had to buy a new blender after that."

"I didn't know how to use the machine. I can learn."

"What happened?" Deirdre asked.

"She was mixing a drink for Samyaza and didn't secure the lid on the blender. She also didn't attach it to the base properly."

Lilith pouted her lip. "It was only a small explosion."

Eve smirked. "I had to clean sticky daiquiri mix off the ceiling...*after* I calmed Sam down and convinced him not to bludgeon you."

Lilith sighed. "Do you see what I mean, Dee? Everything I touch turns to disaster, including my supposed soulmate. Ugh." She dropped her head back on the chair. "He's a cinnamon roll, just like you said I needed."

Deirdre leaned her elbows on her knees. "What's he like?"

Her lips curved upward against her will. "He's handsome. A cameraman for an adventure show, so his job must be exciting. He was charming, sweet, and funny...until he found out who I am."

Eve smiled. "Holy hellhounds. You like him."

"I did. I don't anymore."

"Yes, you do," Deirdre sang.

She huffed. "Only because Venus said he was my soulmate. If she hadn't told me that, I'd have already forgotten about him. But I can't stop thinking about how much I enjoyed his company, and how royally I screwed up yet again. *If* soulmates exist, that means fate tossed me a bone and I buried it in the graveyard without even getting to the marrow."

"Oh no. No way." Dee scooted to the edge of the

couch and held up a finger. "One: You didn't screw anything up. You didn't lie about your identity; he didn't connect the dots. That's on him. Two: If you feel that strongly about him, why don't you dig up that bone and put it where it belongs?"

"Right. Let me hunt down a man who doesn't want anything to do with me and grovel for acceptance." Her body shuddered from simply saying the words. "That would go against my very nature. Besides, I don't have his number."

"Suffering centaurs, Lil. You have got to get better at checking your messages. Where's your phone?" Eve shot to her feet and grabbed the device from the kitchen counter before shoving it toward her. "I've been texting and calling for a day and a half. He came back for you."

"What?" Her heart slingshotted into her throat, and her mouth hung open, her grip on the phone so light, the device slipped into her lap. The sapling Venus's seed had become grew into a flower of hope, its petals fluttering against her ribs as it bloomed.

Lilith swiped open her message app and read the thread from her friend. "He wants to apologize?"

Eve pulled a bar napkin from her pocket and offered it to her. "He left his number with the topside barista Thursday morning. I called you the second I found out."

Her hand trembled as she reached for the napkin. Why in Lucifer's name was her body reacting this way? Her breath caught at the sight of Spencer's handwriting, his name neat and small, his number slightly larger, and the words *I want to apologize. Please call me.* written at the bottom.

"Well?" If Dee scooted any farther forward, her ass would be on the floor. "Aren't you going to call him?"

Lilith folded the napkin in half and swallowed the strange thickness that had formed in her throat. "I don't know."

"What do you mean you don't know? You like him, right?" Deirdre asked.

"From the half-hour conversation I had with him, yes. But can you really get to know someone in thirty minutes? Maybe I should leave it be."

Eve growled low in her throat. "I love you, Lil, but right now, I'd like to smack you. Tell me… Did you feel a spark when you met him? An electricity in your chest that intensified when you touched?"

"Well, yes." The remnants of the magic still rippled slightly beneath her skin.

"Have you ever felt anything like that before?"

"No." Not that she could recall, but she'd been around for millennia. She could have forgotten.

Eve slapped her palm on the arm of the sofa. "He's your soulmate. That was your body's way of telling you, so your mind didn't get in the way of fate."

Lilith pressed her lips into a hard line. Her friends knew what she thought about the soulmate concept, yet they insisted on pushing the idea. She wanted to be annoyed, to snap back with a salty remark, but that damn hope flower had grown so big that her chest felt like it was stuffed with cotton. No, cotton candy. The feeling was way too sweet.

"Do you really think it's possible? That after all these millennia, fate decided it's my turn?"

"Definitely." Deirdre nodded emphatically. "I never thought it would happen to me, and Azrael...he's been around as long as you, right? If it can happen for the Angel of Death, why not for the Queen of the Night?"

"Venus is never wrong when it comes to matters of the heart," Eve said.

Could it be true? Sweet Persephone, why did she so badly want it to be? "If we're soulmates, why did he walk out on me?"

"Remember what I said about your mind getting

in the way of fate?" Eve asked. "Sounds like that's what happened to him. Fate may have deemed you a match, but it's never easy."

Dee laughed. "No kidding. You both have to get out of your own ways and let it happen. Stop fighting it."

Stop fighting. She could do that. If it meant saving Esther's existence, she would do whatever it took. What other choice did she have? Before she could change her mind, she dove head-first into the soulmate concept and dialed Spencer's number. It went straight to voicemail.

"Devil damn it. He's out of the country filming a show." She dropped her phone on the coffee table and bit her lip. She'd waited too long. If she hadn't been wallowing in self-pity and had checked her fucking messages, she could have seen him before he left. "Who knows how long he'll be gone? Esther could be dead by the time he gets back."

"Do you know where he is?" Dee asked.

"He said he was going to Costa Rica. We didn't have time to discuss exactly what they were looking for. He could be anywhere in the country."

Eve grinned slyly. "You know Venus can find anyone when soulmates are involved."

Her sluggish pulse kicked into as close to a sprint as was vampirically possible. "You're right. She can."

"And you've got an all-access pass to come and go from The Underworld to anywhere in the world."

Lilith smiled so big, her cheeks ached, and she shot to her feet. "If you'll excuse me, ladies, I need to pay the Goddess of Love a visit. I'm going to get my man."

CHAPTER SIX

The long dirt road seemed to stretch on forever beneath the moonlight. Thick forest grew on either side of the path, encroaching, almost suffocating, and brimming with wildlife of the deadliest variety. Venomous spiders, poison dart frogs, and bullet ants with a sting that felt like a flaming railroad spike being pounded into your body were only a few. Then there were the snakes... The Costa Rican coral snake, the eyelash viper. Spencer shuddered. Sweet Satan, how he hated snakes.

He and *The Hunt for Cryptids* crew had no intention of venturing into the woods on this expedition, and the snakes and insects preferred the cover of trees to the open road where they set up. Half a mile from the nearest town, there was only one predator they were concerned about tonight.

"This looks like as good a spot as any." Alan pulled a mirror from his pocket and checked his hair. "Ready to roll?"

"I'm going to fly over the area first, make sure no jaguars are waiting to make us a meal." Spencer set his camera down before turning in a circle to check for humans. This far out, this late at night, they had plenty of privacy. But he never took chances when it came to exposing himself as a shifter.

"Pfft." Alan waved a hand. "I can take a jaguar any day."

"Well, I can't," Rebecca said. "Thanks for looking out for us, Spence."

"My pleasure." He called on his owl, and magic buzzed across his skin before filling his core and morphing his body.

Taking to the sky, he soared over both sides of the forest, circling the area and using his enhanced vision to scan the trees and forest floor. A jaguar's coloring helped to camouflage it, but the eyes always glinted in the moonlight.

He spotted plenty of prey, and his owl begged to hunt. But he'd have time for that after the filming. A crow cawed from a nearby tree, and Spencer flew toward it, perching on a branch above it. He tilted his head, eyeing the animal. *Strange.* Crows weren't native to this area.

"Hey, Spencer," Alan called, an odd lilt in his voice. "You've got company."

The crow squawked and shot into the night, and Spencer returned to his friends. *Holy hell.* He landed on the side of the road, and Lilith squatted beside him, her smile brightening her entire face. The same electrical sensation he'd felt in his soul the first time he met her buzzed in his core, and though he tried to stop it, the *hoot* reverberating in his throat sounded way too much like the word *mine* in his head.

"Your owl is beautiful." The sound of her voice made his stomach flutter as if he'd sprouted a second pair of wings, only they were inside his body.

Oh, no. This was not happening. What in hell's name was *she* doing here? And why was his body…his owl…reacting this way yet again? She was a fucking vampire, for Dracula's sake. He shifted to human form and smoothed his t-shirt down his chest, determined to squelch the unwanted emotions awakening within.

"Lilith," he said curtly.

She flinched as she rose, her smile wavering for a

split second before she straightened. "Spencer. I got your message."

Alan cleared his throat, flashing a *what the fuck is going on* look.

Spencer turned his palms upward before focusing on Lilith. "What are you doing here? How did you get here?"

"Your message said you wanted to apologize. I tried the number you left, but it went straight to voicemail. I didn't know how else to reach you, so I came to find you. As for how I got here…magic, of course. There's more than one way in and out of The Underworld."

"You live in The Underworld?" Rebecca gaped.

"I do."

"Sweet! I'm Rebecca." She shoved her hand toward Lilith, who accepted the shake.

"Nice to meet you." Lilith turned to Alan. "And you must be Bigfoot, the star of the show. I'm Lilith."

"You… Uh…" For the first time in Alan's life, he was speechless.

Lilith cast her gorgeous grin toward Spencer, and his breath caught in his throat. "I'll hear that apology now, so we can move forward with our relationship."

"Relationsh—" His nostrils flared with his exhale. He could not have this conversation right now. "I'm working, Lilith. Text me your number, and we can talk about this when I get home."

She flinched again, and she gazed upward, her brow pinching as her lips puckered. Why the hell did he find her expression so damn adorable? It was her magic. It had to be. Lilith was a seductress, and he wasn't about to become her next victim.

That was what he told himself, but when her gaze met his again, something snapped inside him, and warmth bloomed in his belly before rising to his chest. She'd gone to a lot of trouble to find him. The least he could do was offer the apology she deserved.

"Give us a second, guys?"

Alan looked from Lilith to him. "Sure thing." He nodded in the opposite direction, and Rebecca followed him down the road, leaving Spencer alone with Lilith.

She smiled tentatively before catching her bottom lip between her teeth. That little flash of fang sent blood pooling in his groin, which was *so* not the reaction he should have been having. Spencer did not date vampires. Hell, he'd be happy if he never dated anyone again.

"I'm sorry for leaving the way I did." With his arms by his sides, he tapped his index fingers against his thumbs, hoping the single sentence would suffice and she'd be on her way.

She simply arched a delicate brow, and he drew in a breath, grasping for the right words that would convey his sincerity without giving her the idea he was interested. Because he wasn't interested, and he would keep telling himself that until he believed it. Besides… While it was flattering that she tracked him down, the fact she was able to pull it off proved she had power and sway in The Underworld. No telling what kind of magic she used to locate him.

"I'm sorry for being rude, but I'm not interested in dating anyone. I told you that from the beginning."

"Then why did you ask if I was free the next day?"

"I lost myself for a moment. When I found out who you are, it snapped me back into the present, and…even if I was interested in dating, I don't go out with vampires. No offense."

She crossed her arms, her expression turning from amused to curious to baffled. "Why not? It's the blood drinking, isn't it? Do you faint at the sight of blood?"

"No, it's not that at all. Vampires are hunters; so are owl shifters. It's…the whole bit about you being immortal and me having the lifespan of a human." He shrugged. "I can't get past it."

"That's a minor issue that's easily remedied."

"I don't want to be a vampire."

She rested a hand on her hip. "I see."

"I'm sorry you came all this way for an apology, but that's all I have to offer. I should have explained things, and I didn't. Now, I've got to get back to work. I assume you can find your way back home?"

She straightened her spine, lifting her chin slightly. "That's not all I came for."

Why was she making this so hard? "You seem like an amazing woman, but—"

"No." She held up a finger. "Let me finish."

He looked down the road at his friends, silhouetted against the moonlight. Alan tipped back a beer, already preparing for the show.

"I have a problem, and I think you can help me." The crow he'd seen earlier swooped down from the sky and landed on Lilith's shoulder.

"Don't tell me you have some kind of power over birds." If that were the case, he needed to fly as far away from her as possible. She was already mesmerizing without using any magic at all.

"Of course not. This is Percival, my familiar."

He nodded at the crow. "Nice to meet you."

"My other familiar is at home, and she's fallen ill because of me. I didn't want to tell you this, but I, the Queen of the Night, have become a homebody. Esther is lethargic, and she has lost her color, and if I don't add some excitement into my life...if I don't find a purpose soon...she'll die."

Spencer looked at Percival, the crow's onyx feathers glinting blue in the moonlight, and his stomach tightened. He knew a few witches with familiars, and the animals were more than pets. They were an extension of the person.

"I didn't know vampires had familiars." He stroked the back of his index finger down Percival's chest. Lilith's breath caught, and he jerked his hand away.

"Lucifer created them to be my companions in the early years of my curse. I was the only vampire in the world for quite a while." Her gaze grew distant as if the memory were painful. "Please, Spencer, I don't know what else to do."

"How can I help?"

"Let me stay. Let me watch you film your show. I'm sure being near you—" She pressed her lips together. "Being near the excitement will help. It has to."

He drew a breath, taking in Lilith's attire. She wore solid black, her long-sleeved shirt and pants form-fitting, accentuating every curve. Her black ankle boots had a rugged sole and low heel, and though it was ninety degrees and more humid than Hades' asshole, her brow hadn't even begun to glisten with sweat. *Must be nice.*

"I'm dressed for adventure." She flashed her thousand-watt smile, and his heart felt like it stuttered. It didn't, of course. The muscle responsible for pumping blood through his body wouldn't malfunction due to a beautiful woman, but the sensation was a warning sign…one he was about to choose to ignore.

He returned the smile. "You're dressed to rob a bank."

"Maybe we can do that tomorrow?"

He laughed. "All right, you can stay." How could he turn her away when an animal's life was on the line?

"Thank you, Spencer. You have no idea how much this means."

"Stay out of the frame. Just stand behind me and keep quiet."

"You won't even know I'm here."

Oh, he would know. Simply being in the vicinity

of Lilith made his blood hum and his owl flutter beneath the surface. The woman was magnetic...and dangerous.

CHAPTER SEVEN

Percival took to the sky in search of a snack, and Lilith stood behind Spencer like he asked. The scent of his coppery blood pulsing through his veins made her mouth water. She stepped closer, taking in the bouquet of his skin—warm and woodsy—and his pheromones flared with his desire. *Delicious.*

He felt their bond. Of that, she was certain, but Spencer was fighting it. Her friends had assured her this was normal, especially for a topside dweller, and while Lilith would have preferred to declare them soulmates the moment his eyes met hers so they could cut through all the crap, Eve had insisted Lilith let him come to the realization on his own.

She moved closer as Spencer hoisted his camera onto his shoulder, and his pulse quickened, his blood flowing more rapidly through his arteries. She should have fed before she came. The last thing she needed was to chomp on him or one of his friends. He already had a mild disdain for her kind, which drove a stake into her plans for the elusive happily ever after. This would be harder than she thought.

She stepped back and cleared her throat. "What are we hunting?"

"Alan's about to explain." He turned on his camera's light and pointed it at the host.

"*El Cadejos*..." Alan said. "A ghostly canine who's said to have long, black fur, red eyes, and the teeth of a jaguar. According to legend, if you're out late at night...especially if you're drinking..." He held up his beer bottle. "You'll hear the sounds of chains dragging the ground and the clip-clop of *El Cadejos'* goat hooves as he approaches you from behind."

Lilith held in a laugh. It was no wonder they never found any evidence on this show. They were hunting fables. *El Cadejos* was made up by a creative alcoholic who needed an excuse for why he stumbled home at three in the morning, missing his pants and a shoe.

"If *El Cadejos* shows himself to you, it's a sign you need to change your life." Alan downed the contents of his bottle. "Tonight, I'm taking on the role of a drunk to see if we can catch the beastly spirit on camera for the first time."

Oh, dear. Lilith bit her lip. The most they were likely to find out here was light reflecting off the eyes of a jaguar stalking them from the trees.

"And, cut." Alan waved a hand, and Spencer and Rebecca lowered their cameras. "Rebecca, you'll focus on me as I wander down the road. Spencer, you keep your lens trained on the trees. We're looking for anything that moves."

"What will you do if you actually get *El Cadejos* on film?" Lilith asked. "You said you would never expose a cryptid."

"Ghosts don't count," Spencer said.

"They exist on a different plane, so we wouldn't be exposing their home to anyone," Rebecca added.

"If we can catch *El Cadejos*," Alan said, "even if the footage is low light, we'll have something to show the network. They want evidence, and spirits are something we can actually show them."

Except, the spirit they were chasing didn't exist. Lilith drummed her fingers against her thigh as a plan hatched in her mind. "I think I can help. If you want the spirit on film, I can make that happen."

"Can you summon it?" Alan asked, his brow creeping toward his hairline.

Excitement bubbled in Lilith's belly. This would be so much fun. "Something like that. Start recording. I'll be back."

"Where are you going?" Spencer asked.

"You'll see." Lilith spun toward the trees and took off at vampire speed. Even with her new friends' enhanced senses, she doubted they saw much more than a blur as she entered the woods and hid behind a massive trunk.

Her sluggish pulse tried to sprint again, and her smile made her cheeks ache. She couldn't wait to see the look on Spencer's face. No way would the network cancel their show after this.

Picturing what she assumed *El Cadejos* would look like in her mind, she activated her glamour. Magic shimmered around her, transforming her image into a black sheepdog with hooves for feet and fiery red eyes. She didn't shapeshift per se. Her body didn't transform, but anyone looking at her would see the spirit dog, thanks to the magic surrounding her.

She started toward the road but paused. Her guise was too good. Shows like this never found exactly what they were looking for; they only found evidence of it. If she appeared looking precisely like *El Cadejos*, it wouldn't be believable. She called on her magic again, blurring the illusion she'd created and making the sheepdog look more like a black misty blob with eyes. Flash this image on screen a few times, and viewers would fall off their comfy couch seats.

With her new guise in check, she prowled through the forest toward the team. Rebecca filmed Alan while he spun the tale of a local who claimed to have seen the ghostly beast. Spencer panned his camera left and right, scanning the woods for signs of spirit life.

Lilith stepped out from behind a tree, and Spencer froze. She ducked her head, shifting the image to look as if the dog blob were preparing to pounce, and he mouthed the words *holy shit* before shouting, "Alan!"

The host spun toward Spencer and then followed his gaze to the forest. "No fucking way."

Lilith held in a giggle as she imagined the *bleep* that would replace Alan's curse. She slipped back into the trees and reappeared closer to him.

"Are you getting this?" He looked at the beer bottle in his hand and dropped it on the ground.

"Yeah," both Spencer and Rebecca replied, excitement in their voices.

Lilith let out a howl before darting back into the woods and dropping her glamour. That was enough "evidence" for one show. She returned to the road and found Spencer reviewing the footage on his camera while Alan beamed into Rebecca's lens, rambling on about how exciting it was to see *El Cadejos* and how it must be time for him to change his life.

Spencer smiled as she approached, and she rested a hand on his shoulder and peered at the tiny screen attached to his camera. "How did I do?"

He laughed, unbelieving. "I had no idea you could summon ghosts. That was amazing."

When his eyes met hers, a thousand butterflies came to life inside her stomach. If not for her phone buzzing in her pocket, the magnetism between them would have pulled her in, and her lips would've been planted on his without a second thought. Instead, she said, "I can't," and pulled out her phone.

She swiped open the messaging app and found a text from Deirdre: *Esther ate her dinner! Whatever you're doing, keep it up!*

Lilith smiled. She couldn't remember the last time she felt so alive, and the man standing next to her was the reason why. Soulmate or not, she couldn't deny her attraction to him.

"What do you mean you can't?" Spencer's honey-smooth voice pulled her from her thoughts. "How else did you get the spirit to show itself?"

"The only beings I can summon are my familiars."

She held up a hand, and Percival swooped down to perch on her fingers. "I used my glamour to appear in the form of the dog."

The awe that had occupied Spencer's eyes vanished as his expression fell. "You faked it."

Lilith's smile faltered. "I had to. *El Cadejos* is a myth. You wouldn't have found any evidence at all."

He slammed the camera screen shut and squared his shoulders at her, his right eye twitching as he ground his teeth. "We never do."

"Which is why your show is about to be canceled." Was he mad at her? Surely she was misreading the irritation his body language implied. His stiff back and protruding neck tendons didn't mean he was upset. "I was trying to help."

He gave his head a tiny shake and looked at his friends. "Alan, Rebecca, you might as well stop. That was Lilith in the woods."

"Really?" Alan strode toward them, smiling and not exhibiting the slightest bit of the anger radiating from Spencer. "Damn, your glamour is next level."

"It's top level." She shrugged.

"Yeah, it is." Alan held up a hand to high-five her. "That was awesome. Smart not to tell us ahead of time. Our reactions were one hundred percent authentic."

Spencer glowered. "We don't fake evidence on this show. We'll lose credibility."

"It was just a little fake," she said. "I made the image blurry so skeptics could call it a play on light and shadow."

"A little fake is still fake." Spencer shook his head harder and nearly stomped toward the black van parked a few yards up the road.

Well, wasn't that fangtastic? Lilith had screwed up yet again, and this time, she'd pissed off her supposed soulmate. Dee wasn't kidding when she said happily ever afters didn't come easy.

Rebecca chewed her bottom lip, and Alan raked a hand through his hair.

"I'm sorry. I was only trying to help." Lilith tipped her head back and stared at the moon. A wispy cloud stretched across the lower half, and stars twinkled around it, much brighter than the few visible in L.A.

"I thought it was rad," Alan said before jogging toward the van.

Lilith watched as Alan said something to Spencer, who shook his head and threw his arms into the air before handing Alan a memory card. If she wanted to, she could have listened to their conversation. Vampires, especially old ones like Lilith, could hear things a mile away. She didn't dare, though. No doubt what Spencer had to say about her would cut like a pair of fangs to the jugular.

"I should go," she mumbled. "It was nice meeting you, Rebecca."

"You don't have to leave. Spencer's just…" She pursed her lips and stepped closer. "He's been blacklisted in Hollywood. This job is the only one he can get, so he takes it very seriously."

"Blacklisted? What does that even mean? How did it happen?"

"It's a long story that isn't mine to tell. He and Alan have been friends forever, and that's the only reason he's here. He can't get a job in movies or TV anywhere else."

"Oh, my. Who did this to him?" A strange protectiveness burned in Lilith's gut, the desire to find the person responsible and teach them a lesson making her fangs ache and her mouth water.

"His ex-fiancée, but don't tell him I told you. He doesn't like to talk about it."

"A woman ruined his career, and another woman ruined this episode." Lilith rubbed her forehead. She had to make amends.

"I don't think you ruined it, and neither does Alan. Come on, let's go talk to them."

She walked with Rebecca toward the van. The back doors were open, and Spencer leaned against the bumper, his arms crossed. He glanced at Lilith and looked away, but in the split second of eye contact, an array of emotions crossed his features.

"I think we should use the footage," Alan said.

Spencer sighed heavily. "How can a show like *The Curse of Oak Island* run for nine seasons? They've been hunting for the same treasure for years, and they haven't found jack."

"But they have." Lilith stood near Spencer, and his posture relaxed. He uncrossed his arms and rested his hands against the bumper. *Thank goodness.* The idea of him being mad at her sat like a load of garlic in her stomach.

She continued, "They've found bits of wood, coins, tools. I think they even found a piece of jewelry. It's the little things that keep viewers glued to the TV. Intermittent rewards, like a slot machine. Not to mention the curse. Will someone on the show have to die on the island before they can find the treasure?"

Spencer arched a brow. "Sounds like you're a fan."

"I've seen every episode."

Rebecca nodded. "Let's see the footage."

Alan inserted the memory card into a computer on a table in the van, and they all climbed inside to watch. Just as Lilith had wanted, her image was distorted, hazy. Viewers could see what they wanted to see in the black shadow peering through the trees.

"We should use it," Rebecca said.

"It's fake." Spencer sank into a chair.

"Is it, though?" Rebecca sat next to him. "I mean, Lilith is a cryptid. We caught a supernatural being on camera, and that's what our show is about."

Alan nodded. "Our reactions are real. Technically, it's not faked at all. I can do a voice-over at the end, questioning what we saw. Was it *El Cadejos*? Another ghost? A shapeshifter? A *vampire*?"

"The network execs are all human," Rebecca said. "They won't care what it is, only that we caught *something*."

"They're going to cancel us otherwise, and then what?" Alan nudged Spencer with an elbow. "Move back to Arizona and work at the family feed store?"

Spencer closed his eyes for a long blink. "You're right. We're desperate enough, so let's use it." He squared his gaze on Lilith. "But don't ever pull a stunt like that again."

Lilith drew an X over her heart and held her fingers up in a V. "Vampire's honor."

His brow rose in a slow arch. "Is that even a thing?"

"It is now." Lilith winked and stepped out of the van.

"Let's head back to the motel," Alan said as the others filed onto the road. "If the Wi-Fi is decent enough, I'll send the footage to the editors tonight." He and Rebecca climbed into the front seats, leaving Lilith alone with Spencer at the back of the van.

Spencer's lips were tight, his expression a glower, and he shoved his hands into his pockets.

"Thank you for letting me hang out tonight," she said. "It was fun."

A grunt was his only response.

"Why are you still mad at me? I swear I only wanted to help."

He sighed heavily. "I'm not mad at you for trying to help. What you did was dangerous. Do you know how many venomous snakes and spiders live in those woods? Hell, even the frogs are poisonous. You could have been hurt."

How cinnamony-sweet. He was concerned for her safety. She grinned and playfully punched him on the shoulder. "Oh, Spencer. You do care."

"Of course I care. What we do is dangerous enough. You don't need to put yourself at risk for a TV show."

"You're forgetting one tiny detail… I'm immortal.

I could lick a dozen poisonous frogs, and I'd be just fine."

"That's something I can't forget, and it's why this ends now. You and I can never be, and you can't keep showing up on our excursions. You'll have to find your excitement somewhere else."

"But we're…"

"I can't, Lilith. I won't."

The sting of rejection backhanded her across the face, but she maintained her composure despite her thickening throat and sour stomach. "I understand."

Spencer headed to the van. He opened the side door, but before he got in, he turned to her. "I hope your familiar feels better now."

She nodded, and he climbed inside, sliding the door shut behind him. *Ouch.*

CHAPTER EIGHT

Spencer wiped his clammy palms on his pants and adjusted his tie. The last time he attended a meeting with the network execs, he was fired and blacklisted within five minutes of sitting down. He could still see Isabella's smug, wicked grin as she told them she refused to work another day with him on the set.

She'd made up stories about his competence, blamed every mishap on him, called him lazy and self-serving. He'd defended himself, but she had every producer, director, and editor wrapped around her pristinely manicured finger, so he hadn't had a chance.

"That's a scowl I haven't seen on your face in a

long time." Alan sat next to him at the massive oval table, drawing him from his thoughts.

"Thinking about the last time I was here." He poured a glass of room-temperature water from the pitcher on the table and took a sip. It did nothing to relieve the dryness in his throat.

Floor-to-ceiling windows lined the far wall, providing an outrageously expensive view of the city sprawling out twenty stories below. The tint on the glass helped keep out the heat, but it didn't stop sweat from beading on Spencer's forehead.

If their show was canceled, Alan and Rebecca could work elsewhere. Spencer was screwed, thanks to his ex-fiancée. Alan joked about Spencer having to move back to Arizona and work at his dad's feed store, but that was the most viable option he had. He'd blown through his savings keeping himself afloat after the Isabella fiasco. The best he could do would be to move in with his dad, save for a few years, and then head to New York or maybe Austin. Texas would be more affordable.

"I was going to say, 'sorry I'm late,' but since we're the only ones here…" Rebecca forced a smile and sat on the other side of Alan.

"Their time is important, not ours." Alan clasped his hands on the table, squeezing and releasing, squeezing and releasing. "Remember, Spence. If they ask about *El Cadejo*, it was *not* faked," he whispered.

His teeth made an audible click as his jaw clenched. "Right." A little white lie was better than loading customers' trucks with fertilizer. That shit stank. He had to remember that.

Two men and a woman in dark, tailored suits and expensive shoes filed into the room and sat across from them. The woman he recognized as Mary Hinojosa, the head of all programming for the Adventure Channel. The men, one blond, one brunet, both with permanent frowns, he'd never seen.

"Thank you for joining us today," Mary said. As if they had a choice. "We're here to discuss the future of *The Hunt for Cryptids*. As you know, your ratings have steadily dropped over the past year."

Alan straightened and moved his hands to his lap. "We are aware, but we have some ideas to liven up the show."

Did they? That was news to Spencer.

"Have you seen the most recent footage we submitted?" Rebecca asked. Spencer kept his mouth shut, which, as the new guy, he could thankfully get away with.

"The cave-in?" Blondie asked.

"No," Rebecca said. "I mean—"

Mary held up a hand. "While Spencer's near-death experience did add excitement to the show, you still didn't discover a single shred of evidence that the so-called demons you were hunting exist."

Spencer inhaled, ready to point out that the show was called *The* Hunt *for Cryptids*, not *The* Finding *of*, but he thought better of it. It had taken a buttload of sweet-talking on Alan's behalf to convince Mary to allow Spencer on the team. He wasn't about to look a gift network exec in the mouth.

"So you haven't seen *El Cadejo*?" Alan folded his hands on the table. "It must still be in editing. May I make a call and have them send it up? I think you'll like what you see."

The brown-haired man leaned over to whisper something into Mary's ear. She rolled her eyes, shaking her head like she couldn't believe she was about to allow it. "Tell them to email me a link within five minutes."

"Thank you, ma'am." Alan grinned and dialed his phone. "Hey, Joe. I need you to send the *El Cadejo* evidence to Mary Hinojosa right now." He tightened his mouth as he listened to Joe's response. "I know it's not ready. Send what you've got of the sighting. Just that clip is fine. Thanks, man." He returned the phone to his jacket pocket.

A minute later, Mary's pinged.

"You've got mail," Alan said.

Mary held the phone, and the other execs leaned in to view the scene. Spencer closed his eyes, remembering the way Lilith had appeared through the trees. She'd looked every bit the phantom dog with her glamour activated. His heart thumped a hard beat. Without it, she was the most beautiful woman he'd ever seen.

The moment he'd returned to a city big enough to have cell service, her apology text had come through. She seemed genuinely sorry she had tricked them, and she assured him for the umpteenth time she was trying to help. Warmth spread through his chest at the thought of her, so he shifted in his seat, giving his head a little shake to chase the sensation away. The last thing he needed was to get the warm fuzzies for the cold undead.

"Well…" Mary put the phone on the table. "Color me impressed. That's some extraordinary footage. Any idea what it was?"

Alan cut his gaze to Spencer before speaking. "I recorded a voiceover presenting multiple possibilities."

"Such as?" She steepled her fingers.

"A ghost, a shapeshifter, a vampire. You know, the usual."

Rebecca fought a smile, and Spencer ground his teeth.

The blond guy whispered something to Mary, and she nodded before saying something under her breath to the brunet. The man nodded in agreement, and Mary folded her arms on the table.

"We called you here today prepared to inform you your show would be canceled."

The thickness in Spencer's throat turned into a lump the size of a tangerine. Rebecca swallowed hard, and Alan held his breath.

"However, in light of your most recent expedition and the fact we don't have another show lined up, we're going to give you a second chance. I'd rather not fill your timeslot with reruns."

"Thank you, ma'am," Spencer finally spoke. "We won't let you down."

"I hope you're right. One more expedition. You have two weeks to plan it, one week to execute it, and one more for editing. That will be all."

Spencer filed out of the conference room with his friends and stepped into the elevator. The last time he walked this path, the doors sliding shut had felt like the lid of a coffin closing on him, ending his career. This time, he had hope, but…

"Whatever we do, it's got to be epic." He pushed the button for the fourth floor.

"Got any ideas?" Alan asked.

Apparently, no one did because they remained silent the rest of the way down. When the doors opened on their floor, Rebecca led the way to the team's small office. The dark, windowless room was more like a storage closet, but hey, at least they had a computer and enough space to store their camera equipment. *The Hunt for Cryptids* didn't have the ratings to earn them a view.

Alan sat behind the computer, and Rebecca and Spencer sat on either side of him. She chewed on her bottom lip and then opened and closed her mouth as if she wanted to speak.

"What's your idea?" Spencer asked.

"I know when we started this show, we wanted the focus to be on the evidence *we* could capture. But what if we reorganized? So many people catch supposed evidence on their phones these days, we could do a call for submissions, interview the people, focus on the legends rather than the actual hunt."

Alan scowled, two lines forming between his brows as he considered her idea. "That's not what we're about."

"Pretty soon, we won't be about anything," she said. "It's time to rethink our strategy."

"You're right," Spencer said. "That's a good strategy for future episodes if we're allowed to continue, but we've only got two weeks to plan this one. Even with Alan's social media reach, it would take time to get enough quality submissions. Then sorting them all, pulling out the good ones… We don't have that kind of time."

"Let's table the idea for now." Alan's fingers clicked on the keyboard, and a schedule of past episodes opened on the screen. "We need something fresh and doable in a short period."

Spencer scanned the list. "We haven't done Bigfoot in a while. It's not fresh, but it's the easiest one to get evidence for. We could go to a different location to change it up."

Alan grimaced. "I hate to say it, but that might be our only option."

"What about the kitsune?" Rebecca asked. "We haven't done that one, and if we take still images, with the shutter speed slow enough, I can wag my tail and create the illusion of having multiple. If we blur the image, it could be ambiguous enough to make skeptics question it."

"But it would be fake," Spencer said. "We got

away with Lilith's *El Cadejo*. If we make that our M.O., we're begging to get busted."

"He's right," Alan said as he opened a web browser. "No faking evidence. We have to be authentic."

They sat in silence, searching their respective devices for ideas, but Spencer couldn't help himself. He swiped open his messaging app and clicked on his text exchange with Lilith. Yes, he'd replied when she'd apologized. It would have been rude to ignore her. And maybe they'd texted a few more times over the week following the expedition in Costa Rica, so what? He hated the idea of any animal suffering, so he had checked in on Esther occasionally.

Lowering his phone into his lap, he read their most recent exchange.

Spencer: *How's your familiar today?*

Lilith: *Not great. She'll eat, but I've yet to see her as energetic as the sitter described her when I was in Costa Rica.*

Spencer: *I'm sorry to hear that.*

Lilith: *It seems one adventure with you wasn't enough to cure her.*

Spencer: *What are you going to do?*

Lilith: *Perhaps I'll try speed dating again.*

His stomach churned as he reread that line. The

idea of Lilith with another man didn't just ruffle his feathers, it plucked them out one by one, making his skin crawl and his muscles tense. He needed to have a come-to-Jesus meeting with his owl because Lilith was off-limits.

So why couldn't he help himself?

Forget the fact she was powerful enough to squash him like a cockroach in his sleep the moment he did something to piss her off. That was a given, but it didn't stop him from fantasizing about the way her soft, pale skin would feel beneath his fingertips. The way her fangs would feel piercing his flesh as he pumped his hips…

He stretched his neck, banishing the thoughts from his mind. She was immortal, for fuck's sake. He refused to get involved with someone who would outlive him for millennia. She'd said that problem had an easy fix, but there was no way in all of The Underworld he'd let her turn him. His cousin Sam had fallen in love with a vampire a decade ago. When she turned him, Sam had lost his owl. A piece of his soul had died with his transformation, and he hadn't been the same since. The thought of losing that much of himself made Spencer want to vomit. No way was he giving up his owl for Lilith…for anyone.

He had never replied to her speed dating statement, and a full twenty-four hours passed before he heard from her again.

Lilith: *Where are you headed next? Somewhere exciting?*

That was another reason he needed to squelch the emotions his owl was forcing on him. Lilith wasn't interested in *him*. She was after excitement so she could heal her familiar. Spencer was simply a means to an end.

Still, he'd been compelled to confide in her.

Spencer: *We might not be heading anywhere. The execs have called a conference, and I have a feeling they might be canceling the show.*

Lilith: *That's awful. Is there anything I can do to help?*

Spencer: *Glamour the execs and everyone watching the program to make them think it's the best show on TV.*

He grinned as he remembered how long the three little dots had bounced on the screen. Way longer than it should have taken for her to type four words.

Lilith: *I can do that.*

Spencer: *I'm kidding. Please don't.*

Lilith: *Let me know if you change your mind.*

"What are you grinning about?" Alan's voice pulled Spencer from his thoughts.

He shoved his phone into his pocket. "Just something Lilith said last night."

"Lilith?" Rebecca's face lit up. "You didn't tell us you were seeing her. How's that going?"

"We aren't seeing each other. We're just talking. Well, texting."

Alan laughed. "What are you? Seventeen? *We aren't dating, we're talking,*" he said in a ridiculous voice. "What are you 'talking' about?" He made air quotes.

Spencer rolled his eyes. "Forget it."

"No, we want to know," Rebecca said. "Do you like her?"

He wasn't about to explain the conflicted emotions undulating in his psyche. Of course, while his friends, being shifters themselves, would be the most likely to understand the man versus beast dilemma, neither of them had ever met someone whom their animal wanted to claim.

"She offered to glamour everyone at the network to make them think ours was the best show they've got."

Alan's brows shot up. "That's not a bad idea."

"It's unethical." Spencer shook his head.

"And icky," Rebecca added. "That's the only thing that bothers me about vampires. How they can make people see things and forget what happened."

Alan closed his laptop. "You didn't seem to mind when Lilith gave us useable evidence for the show."

"That was different. She saved our asses. Plus, I sense good vibes from her. She seems like a friendly, sincere woman."

"Of course she seems that way to you," Alan said. "Isn't she the protector of womankind or something like that?"

Spencer's phone buzzed in his pocket, and, almost as if Lilith had sensed them talking about her, a text lit up his screen: *How did the meeting go?*

He stood and stepped into the hallway while Alan and Rebecca continued their debate about vampires.

Spencer: *Not as bad as I thought. They're giving us one more chance to produce some evidence.*

Lilith: *That's good news.*

Spencer: *It'll be difficult to avoid crossing the line and exposing someone while still showing enough to make the network happy.*

Lilith: *Hang tight. I might have an idea.*

Spencer: *It's fine. We'll figure something out. I was kidding when I suggested you glamour them.*

Lilith: *This won't involve any glamour. I promise.*

CHAPTER NINE

"Are you sure this is the right way to go?" Lilith stared at her phone lying on the table and ran her tongue over a fang. She'd asked her friends to meet her at the local coffee shop. "It seems like it would be a lot simpler if I told him we were soulmates. He would accept it eventually, just as I will." Maybe. She still had a hard time believing that, after all these millennia, fate would create a life partner who refused to date vampires for the cursed Queen of the Night.

But her friends could be quite convincing.

"Absolutely not." Venus looked at her as if she'd grown a second set of fangs. "You are not, under any circumstances, to tell him that."

"Listen to her, Lil," Eve said. "The Goddess of Love knows what she's talking about."

Lilith huffed. "Back me up, Dee. Don't you think…"

Deirdre shook her head adamantly. "If Azrael had told me we were soulmates from the get-go, I'd have turned tail and hauled my undead ass back to New Orleans. He has to figure it out on his own, or it will never work."

"I've never believed in soulmates, and it's crap like this that makes me skeptical still. Why all the games?"

Venus gave her a sympathetic look. "Because hearts are delicate, especially ones that have been broken before."

Surely she was talking about Spencer's heart. His ex-fiancée had been wicked to him. Of course, Adam kicking Lilith out of Eden and having her cursed for all eternity wasn't exactly kind either. Yes, her heart had been broken too, but the scars had hardened it into a block of stone encased in ice and barbed wire. Lilith was anything but delicate.

Anyway, the Goddess of Love was perpetually single, so how could she be the authority on relationships? And Eve…her luck with the man she was made for didn't last much longer than Lilith's. Neither of them had ever experienced the mysterious happily ever after they claimed to help people achieve.

With Esther's life at stake, Lilith had removed the barbed wire from her heart, and in the short time she'd known Spencer, he'd managed to thaw a few layers of ice. But happily ever after? She looked at Deirdre. "Is it worth the hassle?"

"Down to the last drop."

Venus rested a hand on Lilith's. "He *is* your soulmate. I feel it in my blood."

Who was Lilith to argue with blood? "Will you come with me to talk to Lucifer? I don't think he's going to like my idea."

"He'll despise it." Venus grinned wickedly. "But I'm sure we can convince him. I'll meet you at the palace in ten."

Lilith stopped by her house on the way to Lucifer's castle. Esther lifted her head when she offered her a freeze-dried mouse, but the snake's coloring was still yellowish white.

"I'm trying my best, my sweet, sweet danger noodle." She stroked her familiar's smooth scales, and Esther thankfully ate her dinner. Lilith couldn't be sure if it was the excitement of what she was about to offer Spencer or if it was the man himself making her sluggish pulse thrum, but Esther was moving and eating, so she was on the right track.

"Come, Percival." Lilith stepped out the front door, and her crow flew ahead of her toward Lucifer's palace.

The ruler of The Underworld sat behind a massive dark wood desk in his office. His elbows rested on the arms of a high-backed leather chair, and he steepled his fingers as she knocked on the open door. "Come in, Lilith. Venus said you have a proposition for me."

The Goddess of Love sat in one of two black leather chairs facing his desk, and Lilith sank into the other one.

"What can I do for you?" he asked.

Lilith cleared her throat. "I've been around almost as long as you have."

He huffed an incredulous laugh. "Not quite."

She straightened her spine. "Anyway…"

Venus gave her an encouraging nod.

"I've been all over the world, lived through nearly every century, and I have connections with some very old beings topside. People who were around back when humans believed in magic."

"I am aware." He made a circular motion with his hand, urging her to hurry it up.

"I met a man, an owl shifter, who's part of an

adventure show called *The Hunt for Cryptids.* His show is about to get canceled, and…" She pressed her lips together and glanced at Venus, who patted her shoulder and whispered, "Get to the point."

Lilith nodded. "I'd like permission to take him to some of my contacts and to film evidence that magic used to exist, or at least that people fully believed it did."

Lucifer scowled. "You want to expose the topside supes on television?"

"Not expose them. I simply want to show them signs that supes could possibly exist. Spencer and his friends are all supes themselves. They would never actually reveal anyone's magic."

"Magic is kept secret for a reason." He grabbed a pen and a pad of paper. "You said his name is Spencer? Who else works on this show? I'm putting an end to it."

"Lucifer, no." Lilith's chest turned into a trampoline for her heart, which bounced a few times before getting stuck in her throat. Why did she listen to Venus? She should have just done it and dealt with the consequences later. Lucifer wasn't even aware of the show until she opened her big mouth.

"I swear they're not causing any harm. They interview people who believe in cryptids, and then they film themselves trying to find them. The show's host is a sasquatch, and you *know* those are the most elusive beings of all. I just want to help them out so they don't lose their jobs."

"They can find employment elsewhere." Lucifer set his pen down.

"Spencer can't. It's a long story, Luce, but I *need* to help him. Esther's life depends on it."

Lucifer cocked his head and looked at Venus before focusing on Lilith. "Your snake's condition has improved since you met this man?"

"He's her soulmate." Venus crossed her legs, clasping her hands on her knee.

Lucifer let out a deep belly laugh. "You should have led with that. I couldn't for the life of me ascertain why you'd be so intent on aiding a simple shifter. An *owl* at that."

Lilith ground her teeth. There was nothing simple about Spencer, and his owl was the most beautiful animal she'd ever seen. "It's been a hard fact for me to swallow as well, but I can't deny the urge to help him."

"Why doesn't he move to The Underworld with you? Your soulmate won't need employment, just as you don't."

She grimaced. "He doesn't know it yet. He's

fighting the pull, and this is the only way I can get close to him."

He steepled his fingers again. "I see. And which of your contacts do you plan to start with?"

"I want to take them to Andrei." A man she'd turned centuries ago, her old friend lived in a delightfully gothic castle in Romania. Perfect for their show.

Lucifer laughed so hard he nearly busted a gut. Tears welled in his eyes as his body rocked with amusement, and he wiped them away before they could fall. "You want to take your soon-to-be lover to your old lover's home? Dear Lilith, I'm not sure you've thought this through."

She'd considered that when the idea first formed, but they needed something big to keep their show on the air, and Andrei could provide it.

"Very well. You have my blessing." Lucifer waved a hand, dismissing her. "Don't screw this up."

Her jaw tightened. "I won't."

"Actually, if you can fail in grand proportions akin to the apple debacle, you may screw up all you like. It's been a while since I've been blamed for epic debauchery on Earth."

Lilith rose, narrowing her eyes. "Thanks for your permission."

CHAPTER TEN

This was a bad idea. Spencer sat in his car, clutching the steering wheel with one hand and fisting the other on the console. If Alan hadn't been looking over his shoulder when Lilith's text came through, he could have told her no thanks and been done with her.

Instead, Alan had grabbed his arm and said, "Tell her we'll be there."

Texting with Lilith was one thing. A distant thing. When the warm fuzzies started expanding in his chest, he could put his phone down, walk away, and distract himself from the unwelcome emotions. Seeing her face to face again would be an exercise in willpower he wasn't sure he could sustain.

He inhaled deeply, trying to calm his racing heart,

but the damn thing felt like it had grown humming-bird wings. He checked his hair in the rearview mirror, got out of the car, and paced toward The Fang and Flask.

Alan and Rebecca met him at the door, but he couldn't make himself step inside. Now, in addition to the rapid flapping inside his chest, a swarm of angry wasps had taken flight in his stomach. He froze at the entrance, turning on his heel, and Alan slammed into him, making him stumble.

Spencer stepped aside and gestured for them to enter. "You guys go talk to her. I'll wait in the car."

Rebecca flashed a knowing smile. "She wants to talk to *you*."

And therein lay the problem. She'd been texting him all week, asking him questions about himself, showing interest in him, disarming him. He had to keep reminding himself her interest was fabricated. She wanted to go on another expedition, and that was what this meeting was about.

"She's using me."

Rebecca rolled her eyes. "She's *helping* you."

"Her familiar is sick, and she thinks going on an expedition with us will be exciting enough to save her."

"Men can be so dense." Rebecca palmed his

shoulder. "She's a powerful immortal who can do anything she wants. The possibilities for her to find excitement are endless, yet she's *choosing* you. She likes you. Now, wipe the crud out of your eyes and see her for what she really is."

"We have to hear her out," Alan said. "I don't think another Bigfoot sighting is going to be enough to save our show."

Spencer gazed across the horizon. The sun setting behind the buildings painted the sky in shades of deep pink and purple. A car horn blared from the intersection a block over, and a couple stepped around him to enter the bar.

It would be fine. Hear what she had to say and leave. He was a big boy; he could manage that.

"All right. Let's do this." He crossed the threshold and made his way toward the stairs.

His friends followed him down the flight and through the thick, purple velvet curtain. He'd never set foot in The Underworld before; most people hadn't unless they came to this bar. The average topside-dwelling supe couldn't find the entrances to The Underworld, and that was by design. They couldn't have any old being wandering in willy nilly.

He spotted Lilith at a booth along the far wall, and his breath caught. Her long red hair flowed in thick waves over her shoulders, and her pale, flawless skin reminded him of porcelain—fragile, which he was certain Lilith was not.

The hummingbird sensation in his chest settled as his owl took notice of her, and his feet carried him toward her before his mind realized he was moving. He stopped at the table, letting his gaze wander over her form. She wore a black silk dress with thin straps and a matching choker around her neck. When his gaze met hers, her eyes brightened with her smile.

"Good afternoon, Spencer."

His name on her plump, pink lips turned his skin to gooseflesh.

"Hi, Lilith." Her name tasted like honey on his tongue. *Oh, hell.* Whatever her intention with this meeting, he couldn't deny the attraction. Against his better judgment, he slid onto the seat next to her while Alan and Rebecca took the one across from them.

She held his gaze for a moment before turning to his friends. "Thank you for meeting with me."

"We can't wait to hear your idea." Alan leaned his arms on the table. "I'm sure Spencer told you our show is in trouble."

"Yes, he did, and I think I can help."

"Wait." Spencer cocked his head. "How are you

even here with the sun still up? I thought most vampires were dead to the world during daylight hours."

She smiled slyly. "I'm not most vampires."

No kidding. She wasn't even most women. She was gorgeous, smart, and sexy, and she smelled of mint and lavender. Delicious.

"There is no daylight in The Underworld, so I can be awake—and sleep—whenever I choose. It's one of the many perks of living in Lucifer's lair."

"What's it like being in the dark all the time?" Rebecca asked. "How do you keep your body regulated? I think I'd go crazy."

"It isn't dark all the time. Lucifer controls the 'skies' and creates the seasons for us. The Underworld has become quite pleasant since he found his soulmate. We have roads and shops much like you have up top."

"I'd love to see it." Rebecca rested her forearms on the table, leaning forward. It appeared Lilith's magnetic effect wasn't reserved for Spencer.

"Perhaps I can give you all a tour sometime."

"That would be amazing." Rebecca bit her lip. "One more question, and then we can get down to business."

Lilith glanced at Spencer, her gaze dipping to his

mouth before she returned her attention to Rebecca. "Shoot."

"You said you're not like most vampires, so would you burn in the sun? Is that part of your curse?"

"That was two questions." Alan playfully elbowed Rebecca.

"Sorry. I've got a million more."

Lilith pressed her lips together, amusement dancing in her blue eyes. "I'm happy to answer them all. It's been a long time since I've met anyone new." Again she glanced at Spencer, and his throat felt like he'd swallowed a massive cotton ball.

"Sunlight does not affect me the way it does other vampires, and yes, it's part of my curse. I lose my power when exposed to the sun; I get fatigued, but that is the extent of the effect."

"Then why do the others fry?" Rebecca asked.

"The effect the sun has on my children entirely depends on the degree of separation. The further down the line they were created, the less of my magic they received. Vampires that I sire myself can be in the sun for short periods. Likewise, their glamour is nearly as strong as mine."

"Fascinating. How many have you sired?" Rebecca looked like a kid who'd just met Santa Claus.

"This is interesting," Alan said, "but let's talk about your idea for the show."

"Right. I can answer your questions another time." She winked at Rebecca before turning her heart-melting smile on Spencer. "I believe I can help you find evidence that won't expose our kind but will be intriguing enough to get your network's attention."

Spencer angled his body toward her. "We're listening."

"I have a dear friend in Romania, a vampire I sired ages ago, who has access to a gravesite where supposed vampires are buried. He has agreed to let us unearth a grave and film the way they disposed of those suspected of vampirism in the seventeen hundreds."

"You want us to dig up a corpse." Spencer pressed his lips into a thin line. It wasn't the worst idea he'd ever heard. People accused their friends and relatives of being vampires for all kinds of reasons back then. He'd done plenty of research on the subject when they'd tried to get permission to film there before. In fact...

"They used to say a person born with red hair and blue eyes would turn into a vampire. Is that because of you?"

She caught her bottom lip between her teeth, revealing a fang, and blood rushed to Spencer's groin. Never in his life had a vampire's fangs turned him on, but every time he glimpsed Lilith's, he couldn't help but imagine her biting him.

"Guilty." She let out a small laugh. "I didn't mean for the superstition to spread through the villages. I was angry back then, and…" She shook her head. "Andrei lives in a small castle on the outskirts of town. The gravesite is on his property, so we don't have to worry about getting permission from the government. He has even offered us rooms during our stay. What do you think?"

Alan rubbed his thumb and forefinger on his chin, feigning deep thought. "You want us to stay in a Romanian vampire's castle, dig up a grave of someone accused of vampirism, and get it all on film?"

"That's the gist of it," Lilith said.

Alan grinned. "When do we leave?"

"As soon as you're ready." Lilith looked at Spencer, taking in his guarded expression. "What do you think?" She shifted in her seat to face him, her knee resting against his. "I would never force my will on you, so if we do this, we do it together. If you don't want to, just say the word."

He glanced down at where her leg touched his. The small bodily contact lit a fire in his core and raised a red flag so high it flapped in his face. His logical mind told him the fortress he'd built around his heart was beginning to crumble, and he needed to run as far from her as he could. His owl, on the other hand, screamed at him to accept the offer, to tear down the walls and let Lilith in.

Spencer looked at his friends, who both made eyes at him that said they'd murder him if he said no. He could reinforce his defenses. He owed it to his team to do this. "I'm in."

"Yes!" Rebecca shook her fist in victory.

"Let's go work on the logistics." Alan slid out of the booth, and Rebecca followed. "We can probably get a flight out the day after tomorrow. Four tickets?"

Lilith brushed her hair behind her shoulder. "I will meet you there. I'll go a day ahead to help Andrei prepare for your arrival."

"Sounds good," Alan said. "You coming, Spence?"

Spencer didn't budge from his spot next to Lilith. He should have gotten up and hauled ass out the door, but he couldn't force himself to move. This was bad. Very, very bad. "I'll catch up with you later."

Rebecca grinned. "Thank you for this, Lilith. We owe you."

"It's my pleasure." She waved as Alan and Rebecca walked away.

"Why are you doing this?" He clenched his teeth. He knew the reason, but he wanted to hear it from her. Wait…no, he didn't. "Never mind. You're doing it for the adventure, to save your familiar."

She tilted her head, the amusement returning to her eyes. "If I simply wanted an adventure, to see an old friend and dig up a grave, don't you think I could do that on my own?"

Good point. "I suppose you could."

Lilith sighed and rested her hand on the table. "I should be honest with you. The reason I'm helping is that we're…"

She pursed her lips before looking into his eyes. "I've grown fond of you. When I'm near you, I feel things I've never felt before. It's this warm, soft sensation that makes my stomach flutter and my chest tighten, and I like it very much. I enjoy your company, and I want to spend more time with you."

Spencer held Lilith's gaze, searching for any indication of deception. All he found was sincerity. She meant every word. A fissure formed in the fortress around his heart, and the walls crumbled even more. His owl fluttered near the surface, and something in his core burned as an invisible tether formed between them.

Sweet Lucifer's testicles. Was this really happening?

His owl rose up, filling his chest with yearning, whispering in his mind. His stomach turned in a pleasant way, like on the first drop of a rollercoaster, and his skin pricked the way it did right before he sprouted feathers. If he didn't do something soon, he wouldn't be able to stop the shift. The owl had spoken, and the man needed to respond.

Fuck me. "Who." He clamped his mouth shut.

Lilith giggled. "You hooted. That's so cute."

Cute? *Way to go.* He cleared his throat and rested his hand on hers. The feel of her soft skin beneath his fingers sent a jolt of electricity straight to his heart, and whatever was left of the walls came down.

His owl had chosen Lilith as his mate. "I think I might know how you feel."

She narrowed her eyes. "I'm quite certain you don't."

Fuck it. He couldn't fight the connection, so he leaned toward her, slid his fingers into her silky hair, and pulled her face to his. When their lips met, she gasped before melting into him. She scooted closer, taking his face in her hands and slipping out her tongue to brush with his. She tasted like mint and honey, and his owl settled beneath the surface, content with Spencer's decision.

But what decision had he just made? Lilith was immortal. He would grow old and die. She was the mother of all vampires. The Queen of the Night. What made him think a woman like her would allow herself to be tied down to a man like him?

If he told her now that she was his fated mate, she would probably laugh in his face. He would have to earn her trust, prove to her he was a worthy mate.

He brushed his tongue across her upper lip, and she whispered, "Be careful of my fangs."

He didn't want to be careful. He wanted to feel them piercing his skin, to watch her as she drank from him. But not here. There would be time for him to explore everything about this magnificent creature later…and time for him to wrap his mind around the ramifications of what his owl had done. Right now, he simply wanted to hold her.

If he were human, he would call this infatuation, lust, insanity. But when a shifter's animal chose a mate, there could never be another. The man might as well jump on board the crazy train because it was leaving the station with or without him.

She ran her fingers down his arm, squeezing his hand before resting her palm on his thigh. His dick strained against the fabric of his jeans, and as her nails dug into his leg, he groaned.

He broke the kiss, pulling away before things went any further. Of course, Lilith could have glamoured their booth so no one would see them, but the first time he made love to her, it would not be in a public bar. He would take his time with her and make her feel more things she'd never felt before.

Lilith brought her fingers to her lips before she smiled slyly. "Perhaps you do know how I feel. At least partly."

He trailed his fingers down her cheek. "I guess I'll see you in Romania."

She grabbed his hand, lacing her fingers through his. "Would you like to come early with me? We can get there through a portal in The Underworld. It might give us some time to get to know each other better before your friends arrive."

Alan would be pissed that he'd have to handle all the equipment, but Spencer had a feeling Rebecca would be thrilled. Alan would get over it. Owls only ever claimed one mate, and they stayed together for life. His nutjob of a bird had chosen the world's first woman, but as long as she seemed interested, he couldn't deny his instincts.

"I would love to."

Her smile widened. "Meet me here tomorrow afternoon at three."

"It's a date."

"Yes, it is."

CHAPTER ELEVEN

"You have outdone yourself, as always, Arachne." Lilith gazed at her reflection in the mirror at the Black Widow Boutique. The dark blue, magical fabric clung to her curves like a second skin, and as she turned from side to side, the color shimmered like the midnight sky.

"It's UPF one thousand," the spider shifter replied, "and I know you don't like hats, but if you're going to be outside for long, you might consider wearing this." She picked up a matching midnight blue sun hat with a wide brim.

Lilith accepted the item. Arachne created magical clothing for the citizens of The Underworld, and she always knew exactly what her customers needed, even when they didn't know themselves. She put on the hat and the pair of black sunglasses Arachne handed to her.

"You look like a Hollywood star." Arachne clipped a stray thread from the hem of Lilith's shirt.

"Indeed, I do."

"The outfit is missing something, though." Arachne tapped a finger against her lips, and Herbie, her spikey little…well, Lilith wasn't sure what kind of creature he was…skittered across the floor. The size of a house cat, Herbie had four beady eyes, and Lilith counted eight legs, so perhaps he was a spider.

"Of course. How could I forget?" Arachne lifted Esther from her spot on the small sofa and draped her over Lilith's shoulders. "There we go. Totally Lilith."

Percival cawed his approval from his perch, and Lilith stroked her hand down Esther's scales. Her familiar hadn't fully recovered. Far from it, but a washed-out version of her natural color had returned and she was eating, so Lilith brought her on an errand run to spend some time with her oldest friend before she left.

"Spencer is going to want to rip these clothes off you the moment he sees you, but if there's daylight around, you make him wait, understand? You'll need all your strength the first time you do it with your soulmate. It'll be mind-blowing."

Lilith laughed. "I'm sure I can keep him in line." Although, after the heat of their first kiss, she'd be the one wanting to rip clothes off.

The memory played in her mind, and she closed her eyes, relishing it. He had felt their bond; of that, she was certain. He would be her life partner, even if it took him some time to adjust to the idea.

Her heart sank at the thought. His life would be a nanosecond compared to her cursed eternity, and he had made it clear turning him into a vampire wasn't an option.

"Is there something wrong with the clothes? You hate the hat, don't you? Herbie said you'd hate the hat." Arachne snatched it from her head and magically rewove it, tightening the stitches and narrowing the brim.

"No, the hat was fine as it was." She took off the glasses and folded them, slipping them into a magical pocket. The glasses seemed to disappear against her thigh, not disturbing her silhouette in the least. "You would make a fortune if you could sell these clothes topside. Human women would go nuts for pockets like these."

Arachne laughed. "The world isn't ready for that kind of magic."

"Indeed, it isn't." Nor was Lilith ready to have her heart wrenched from her chest in forty years when Spencer's body gave out on him. "Fate has played a cruel joke on me."

Her expression turned serious. "Fate doesn't play jokes on anyone."

"Perhaps I am the exception." She gazed into the mirror at Esther. Cruel prank or no, her time with Spencer was improving her familiar's health. Saving her snake would be worth the heartbreak. "Do you have the other set of clothing I requested?"

"Of course." Arachne handed her a box wrapped in a dark blue ribbon of the same fabric as her clothes.

"Please tell me this outfit doesn't shimmer. Andrei prefers to blend in."

She crossed her arms. "Do you really have to ask?"

"Thank you, old friend." Lilith tucked the box under her arm and strode for the door.

"Don't do anything I wouldn't do," Arachne called as she stepped onto the sidewalk.

Lilith banished the depressing thoughts of Spencer's short life from her mind and delivered

Esther to Deirdre's house before grabbing her suitcase and making her way to the bar.

Spencer sat at the same table as yesterday, and as his eyes met hers, he stood. He wore jeans and a heather gray t-shirt. His light brown hair was styled into a perfect mess, and the corners of his eyes crinkled when he smiled, making her heart thump hard in her chest. The fine hairs on her arms and the back of her neck stood on end, the draw of her soulmate so intense she could hardly bear it.

"You look amazing." He stepped toward her and placed a sweet, tentative kiss on her cheek. He lingered there a moment, his breath warming her skin, and she rested her hand on his cheek, turning his face toward hers.

"How about a proper kiss?" She brushed her lips to his, and her entire body hummed from her core to the top of her head and the tips of her toes.

With a hand on her hip, he tugged her closer, opening for her, his tongue tangling with hers. She closed her eyes and drank him in. Well, it wasn't quite the kind of drinking she'd have liked, but kissing was good for now.

She broke the kiss and caught her bottom lip between her teeth. Spencer's gaze dipped to her mouth, and his pupils dilated. Sweet Persephone, she couldn't wait to taste him. "Shall we go? Andrei awaits."

Spencer blinked as if coming out of a daze. "Yeah." He grabbed a beige duffel bag and slung it over his shoulder. "Didn't you say Andrei was a vampire?"

"I did." She slipped her hand into his and led him out of the bar and into The Underworld.

"Why are we going so early in the day? Aren't you weakest when the sun is out?"

"We are, but my gift for him requires sunlight. And he's hosting a vampire ball tonight for which he must prepare."

"A ball?" Nervous tension tightened his shoulders, and he adjusted his bag.

"Not to worry. No fangs, no ball. You and I will not be attending."

His posture relaxed. "I don't want to keep you from the fun."

"I prefer your company over that of a bunch of crusty, old vampires any day."

"Good to know. Whoa." His eyes widened as he took in the environment. The "sky" appeared as midnight, complete with a crescent moon and twinkling stars, and artificial lights illuminated the streets and the quaint buildings surrounding them.

"First time in The Underworld?"

"Yeah. I know you said it was a village now, but I was expecting at least a little fire and brimstone."

"That's reserved for Hell these days. The damned still get to enjoy the heat." She led him through the center of town and hung a left toward the portal. "This will lead us to Romania. Are you ready?"

Spencer eyed the glittering black abyss that would take them to their destination...with a little help from Lilith's magic, of course. "Is it safe? I'm not going to end up melded with the castle wall, am I?"

"This isn't the Philadelphia Experiment. I've been using portals for millennia."

He leaned away from the gateway.

She pursed her lips and released his hand. "You don't trust me yet. I understand." And why should he? He'd only known her a week, and she wasn't allowed to tell him he was her soulmate yet. "I will take you back to the bar, and you can see if you can catch a flight."

"Actually..." He took her hand again. "I do trust you. It's a feeling I'm not used to, but I do."

Her blood seemed to fizz in her veins, and she smiled. "Good. Percival?" Her crow swooped down and landed on her shoulder. "Shall we?"

He inhaled deeply, looking from her to the portal. "Let's do it."

"You'll feel a little tickle." She tugged him through, the magic of the portal vibrating across her skin a moment before they landed on Andrei's doorstep.

Spencer panted, and his mouth hung open in a most adorable way. He clutched his arms, his legs, the top of his head before muttering, "Holy shit."

"It wasn't so bad, was it?" She set her suitcase and Andrei's gift at her feet.

"That was incredible!" He peered up at the massive castle doors, then turned in a circle, taking in his surroundings. "We're in Romania? Just like that?"

She laughed. "Just like that."

"Is this how you found me in Costa Rica? You walked through a portal, and there I was?" The light in his eyes reminded her of a child the first time he saw the ocean, and her chest gave a squeeze. Everything about him was endearing.

"Venus found you for me, but yes, this is exactly how I showed up on your ghost hunt." She chuckled. "I might have scared the daylights out of your friends at first."

"I can imagine the looks on their faces when you suddenly appeared. I…" He moistened his lips, and that little swipe of tongue made heat pool below her navel. Oh, the places she'd let him lick…

He gazed into her eyes, and she looked back at him, and it felt like they were different poles of a magnet being drawn together by an invisible force that was impossible to resist. This soulmate bind didn't mess around. Hell, she'd have sworn Spencer had glamour magic because the rest of the world seemed to dissolve away until he and she were the only things left in the universe.

She'd never felt like this with Adam. Not once. Not even close. Why in all of Lucifer's realm would her creator force them together yet deny them this bond that she now felt with Spencer? Why would fate make her wait thousands of years to experience what so many already had?

A spark of anger ignited in her chest, and she closed her eyes. The bitterness she'd lived with for millennia expanded in her chest, fanning the flame, but when she looked into Spencer's eyes once more, it was like a firehose blasted in her chest, washing away the resentment. She was with him now, and that was what mattered. *Please, universe, don't let this be a cruel joke.*

The *thunk* of the lock disengaging drew her back to the present, and one of the massive double doors swung open. Andrei stood in the entry, his posture perfectly straight, his hands clasped behind his back. He wore black pants with a deep purple button-up, and his wavy, dark brown hair reached down to his shoulders.

"Welcome." He gestured for them to enter, and Lilith tucked his gift beneath her arm. Spencer picked up her suitcase and carried it into the foyer behind her.

Percival took flight, circling the entry of the castle, which was as big as Lilith's entire house, and he perched on the rail of a grand stone staircase. A chandelier with a million crystals sparkled from above, bathing the room in white light.

Andrei cocked his head, an amused grin spreading across his face. "I expected a thank you gift, but you've outdone yourself, dear friend." He raked his gaze over Spencer, who bristled. "I prefer my main course to be meatier, but he'll make a nice appetizer at our feast tonight."

Lilith laughed and kissed him on both cheeks. "Sorry to disappoint, but this one isn't on the menu. He's the camera operator for the show I told you about."

Spencer's eyes narrowed, his calculating gaze bouncing between Lilith and Andrei. Was that jealousy she sensed rolling off him in waves? She hoped so.

"Pity." Andrei placed his hands on her shoulders and squeezed before dropping his arms to his sides. "Well, welcome anyway."

"Andrei, this is Spencer, my…friend." Was that what she should call him? Or should she have said boyfriend? Lover? Judging by the way Spencer's jaw ticked, friend was most definitely not the right word.

"Always a pleasure to meet a shifter. What's your animal?" Andrei offered his hand, and Spencer slapped his palm into it.

"Owl. Thanks for letting us film here. We appreciate it."

"Anything for Lilith." He lifted his brow and glanced at her. "She is quite special, isn't she?"

"Very," Spencer replied curtly.

Oh, my. Normally, when two men fought over her, she would tell them they could go fuck each other. A woman was not a prize to be won. But seeing Spencer react this way to Andrei's negging made her insides burn in a most pleasant way.

Plus, they weren't really fighting, were they? Spencer was jealous of whatever relationship he perceived between Andrei and her, but he hadn't boldly staked his claim like most men would have.

"Hmm." Andrei regarded Spencer before turning to Lilith. "I do hope you'll join us for the feast tonight. We could…catch up…after."

Okay, it was time she put a stop to this. Andrei sensed her bond with Spencer. She turned him centuries ago, so he could pick up on these things, thanks to the sire/child link. He always loved to needle people, to press their buttons until they snapped. He hadn't changed a bit.

She slipped her hand into Spencer's. "Thank you for the invitation, but I'm going to pass. I'd like to show Spencer the gardens once the sun sets if that won't interfere with your dinner."

"Be my guest." He bowed.

"Speaking of the sun…" Lilith offered him the box. "I had Arachne make you a sunsuit. It's SPF one thousand."

He opened the box and felt the fabric. "It is exquisite. I shall wear it to the market this weekend."

"Do you want to try it out, make sure it works? It would be a bummer to get all the way into town and pass out from the UV rays." She tugged her sunglasses from her magic pocket. "I've got one on too."

Andrei flagged over a servant and handed him the box. "I trust you. If you wanted to destroy me, you'd have done it long ago."

Spencer stiffened at his words, and Lilith squeezed his hand, hoping to reassure him. She would never destroy one of her children unless they turned into a murderous monster. Andrei followed the rules. Murdering and instilling fear in the villagers would make it difficult for him to stay in one place.

"I'm sorry I can't be a better host, but I have business to attend to."

"Thanks for accommodating us on such short notice." Spencer offered his hand to shake once more, and Lilith warmed to him even more.

"Any friend of Lilith's is a friend of mine. Willem." Andrei flagged over his servant. "Show them to their rooms. If your accommodations are lacking in any way, Willem will see to your needs."

Spencer picked up Lilith's suitcase, and Willem took it from his hand. "Right this way."

They followed the young vampire up the stairs and down a long, dimly lit corridor on the second floor.

"For the lady, and for the gentleman." He gestured to two different doors across the hall from each other before setting her suitcase in her room and scurrying away.

Spencer stood in his doorway, tapping his index finger against his leg. "Andrei is an interesting guy."

"He's quite the character. Would you like to see the gardens now? My clothes will protect me from fatigue. We could watch the sunset."

He ground his teeth, considering her offer. "Give me half an hour to get my head straight. This is a lot to take in."

Indeed, it was, and he was handling it splendidly. "Take all the time you need."

CHAPTER TWELVE

S pencer sat on the edge of the bed, holding the bridge of his nose with his thumb and forefinger. Lilith and Andrei used to be lovers. He could tell by the way the Romanian looked at her, an ancient flame burning in his eyes that made Spencer's owl want to gouge the suckers from his face.

Lucky for Andrei—but mostly for Spencer—the man had stayed in control. His rational human mind had reminded him picking a fight with a hundreds-of-years-old vampire would get him killed at best, served up on a spit with an apple shoved in his mouth at the dinner party at worst. Well, he could think of worse things, but that was a path he wouldn't allow his mind to go skipping down. No sense in imagining himself as the star of a horror movie.

Of course, living in The Underworld around all those demons, Lilith was probably used to—expected—men to fight over her. Spencer didn't have it in him to throw the first punch, though. If Andrei started something, he would do his damnedest to finish it, but so far, it seemed the old vampire was just trying to get a rise out of him.

Or had it been a test? Had Lilith orchestrated the encounter to see what kind of man Spencer was? If she was looking for an alpha, she would be disappointed.

Don't be ridiculous, asshole.

Surely a woman of Lilith's age and prominence wouldn't play games like that. She'd either have to accept him as he was or find someone else to toy with. His feathers ruffled beneath the surface at the thought of her finding someone else. No, Lilith had to be his. He would just have to find a way to convince her that she needed a nice guy in her life.

A soft knock sounded from the hallway, and he cleared his throat. "Come in."

Lilith's angelic face appeared as she cracked open the door. "The sun will be setting soon. Would you like to see the gardens now?"

"I'd love to." He followed her through a long corridor lit with electric lamps, their sconces made to look like torches. When Lilith was here the first time, actual torches probably illuminated the hallway…the entire castle. They made a left, another left, and then a right before descending a narrow servants' staircase and exiting onto the back porch.

"You know your way around the castle well."

She pulled the door shut and gestured for him to walk with her. "I lived here for a time when I first turned Andrei. He and I… He needed guidance."

He stopped at the edge of the pavement and fisted his hands, the green-eyed monster trying to claw its way to the surface again. "You were lovers."

She tilted her head, studying his eyes. "Yes, we were."

"And now?"

"I'm here with you, am I not?" She slipped her hand into his and guided him toward a pristine garden with a bubbling stone fountain. A topiary shaped like a wolf stood on one side of the structure, a crescent moon-shaped bush on the other. The sun sank behind the mountains in the distance, the waning light casting a purple glow on the clouds.

Her hand felt cool wrapped in his, and as she twisted her palm to lace their fingers together, warmth spread through his chest. She *was* there with him, and he couldn't think of anywhere he'd rather be.

"Why did you break up?"

She was silent for a moment, her jaw working like she couldn't find the right words. "Times were different then. Even though I sired him, I'm a woman, so I was considered less-than. Andrei was a typical brute of the time, and I enjoyed him for a while. Until he began to assert dominance, to 'put me in my place,' so to speak."

"He wanted to control you."

"Yes, he did."

"I can imagine that didn't go over well."

She shrugged. "All men were like that, but I will never agree to a subservient position in any relationship. No woman should."

"You're absolutely right. I can't imagine trying to dull your shine."

She let out an embarrassed laugh, and if a vampire were capable, she would have blushed. "What about you? Tell me about your life before Hollywood."

"I grew up in Arizona. My mom never married, so it was just her, my sister, and me. When I was old enough to get a job, I worked at my dad's feed store, lugging fifty-pound bags of horse food, keeping the stockroom organized. I stayed there into my late twenties." He laughed. "My life's not nearly as interesting as yours."

"It sounds quaint." She raised her brows. "And absolutely boring."

"It was. I enrolled in the audio/video program at the local community college, learned how to operate a camera, and headed to L.A. to add some excitement to my life. I worked odd jobs on indie shows until I landed a spot on *Expedition Excitement*, and well… Rebecca said she told you the rest."

She nodded. "This blacklist you're on. It makes it impossible for you to find employment in the industry?"

He nodded. "Which is why this expedition is so important. If our show gets canceled, I'll have to move back to Arizona. I don't have any other skills, and lugging feed doesn't pay nearly enough to afford an apartment in L.A."

"I will do my best to provide the footage you need. *Real* evidence. No glamour."

"Thank you." He stopped walking and faced her, resting his hand on her hip. "I mean that."

"It's my pleasure. And I apologize for Andrei's negging earlier. He sensed our bond and was subtly challenging you."

"I figured." Their bond? Could vampires sense when a shifter had chosen a mate? His owl fluttered beneath the surface.

She grinned. "For a moment, I thought you were going to punch him."

"The idea crossed my mind."

"I'm glad you didn't." She brushed her fingers down his arm, the softness of her caress raising goosebumps on his skin. "I rather like the sweetness in you."

His stomach clenched. Of course she did. After her story about Andrei and her experience with Adam, it was obvious. Lilith wanted a partner, an equal. He could be that for her.

He leaned in and brushed his lips to her cheek before gliding them toward her ear and whispering, "Is that so?"

"Mm-hmm." She inhaled deeply and rested a hand on his shoulder. "You are cinnamony sweet."

He closed his eyes and nuzzled into her neck, breathing in her intoxicating scent. He'd been attracted to her from the moment their eyes met, long before his owl staked his claim. The more he got to know her, the harder he fell. Lilith was an amazing woman. Nothing like her reputation. She was the kindest woman he'd ever met.

"Fly with me." Her lips brushed his ear, making him shiver.

He pulled back to look into her eyes. "You can fly?"

She nodded before shrugging one shoulder. "My body can't, but my mind can."

"What do you mean?"

"I can connect with Percival." At the mention of her familiar's name, the crow swooped down and landed on the edge of the fountain. "I see what he sees. Hear what he hears. I can feel the wind through his feathers. It's exhilarating."

"No kidding." He gazed up at the crescent moon and the stars sparkling around it. His owl fluttered near the surface at the thought of soaring beneath the silvery light. "Let's do it."

Lilith's smile sparkled brighter than the stars as she sat cross-legged on a stone bench. Resting her hands on her knees, she closed her eyes and inhaled deeply. Percival cawed and flew to her side, landing on the bench.

"Are you ready?" Her voice felt like music filling his head.

"You can read minds?" He waited for a response, but Percival only ruffled his feathers impatiently.

"Can you read minds?" he asked aloud.

"Sadly, no. I can only send others my thoughts."

Nothing sad about that. He didn't need her nosing around inside his head. "I can't speak in owl form."

"That's okay. We'll simply enjoy the view and the rush of the breeze."

If she hadn't already wormed her way into his heart, this would have done it. He called on his owl, his skin pricking as feathers formed beneath the surface. They sprouted through his pores, and his body morphed into his bird.

Percival…Lilith…flapped the crow's wings and took to the sky. *"Come on, slowpoke."*

Spencer's heart sprinted, and he took off after her, into the night. They soared over the castle grounds, taking in the magnificent gardens from above. Dozens of ornately crafted topiaries in various animal shapes dotted the grounds, and flowers in every color imaginable spread out beneath them.

Light burned in a downstairs window of the castle, no doubt where the bloody dinner party was happening. He was tempted to fly down and perch in the window to see what happened at a soiree like this, but he didn't dare. He'd finally warmed to the idea of being with a vampire. He didn't need to see their blood orgy…or whatever they were doing in there.

"The humans are glamoured," Lilith said as if reading his mind. *"Being bitten is quite a pleasant experience."*

An experience he wanted…needed…to have. *Now.* He returned to the fountain and shifted to his human form before sitting on the bench next to Lilith. She didn't move, didn't breathe. Not that vampires needed to.

She could have been a statue in the garden until a smile tugged at her lips and her eyes fluttered open. "Thank you for that."

"Thank *you*. I haven't had a flying companion since I moved to L.A."

"Companions. Is that what we are?" she asked.

Being this close to her, his entire body hummed with need. "We could be so much more."

She drifted toward him. "I'd like that."

He took her mouth with his, gripping her hip with one hand and cupping the back of her neck with the other. She moaned into his mouth and clutched his shoulders, the sound vibrating into his throat and shocking his heart with enough electricity to send him into cardiac arrest.

His heart didn't stop, but his dick hardened into a rod. He had no clue how a shifter could make a vampire his mate, but right now, he didn't care. He needed her like he'd never needed anything before. "Bite me," he whispered against her lips.

She sucked in a sharp breath and pulled back to look into his eyes. "Are you sure?"

His grip tightened on her hip. "No glamour. I want to feel everything."

"Have you ever been bitten?" Her voice was breathless.

"No, not that I'm aware of."

She let out a slow exhale as if relishing the idea of being his first. "Let's go inside. If your feelings for me are remotely close to mine for you, my bite will lead to other things…things I would rather do in private."

A warm shiver ran through his body at her words, and she took his hand before they darted through the gardens, into the mansion, and up the stairs to her room. Lilith closed the door and shoved him against it, her body melting into his, her lips grazing his neck.

"I've wanted you since the moment I saw you." She trailed her tongue from his shoulder to his ear and nipped his lobe.

His skin turned to gooseflesh. "To drink or to fuck?"

An *mmm* resonated in her throat. "Both…and more."

Sweet Lucifer's testicles, this woman was hot. Her curves fit perfectly against his frame. Her luscious minty, floral scent made his head spin. Her voice was the most beautiful melody to ever reach his ears. She might have been a siren leading him to his death, but at this moment, it didn't matter. He would take pleasure in his demise.

"I care for you, Spencer. Do you care for me?"

"More than you know." He slid his hands down to grip her ass, and she pressed her hips into his.

"Then my bite will be an aphrodisiac, an orgasm in itself. Perhaps we should save it for the end. I'd hate for things to…finish…before we get started."

Good idea. That would be a blow to his small ego he might not recover from. Spencer Monroe, the normal guy who won Lilith's heart, who came in his pants at the first bite. No, thank you.

"Shifters recover quickly, so you don't have to worry about my performance."

"I wasn't trying to say—"

He caught her mouth with his, brushing his tongue against hers before continuing. "But I would like to savor you before you blow my mind."

She flashed a sinful smile. "And I you."

"Besides…" He grabbed one thigh and then the other, lifting her and wrapping her legs around his waist. "Nice guys always finish last in the bedroom. It's the polite thing to do."

He laid her back on the bed and slid his hand from her throat downward, between her breasts to her stomach. She arched into his touch, and he gripped her thighs, positioning himself between them before tugging his shirt over his head.

"Oh, my." Lilith's pupils constricted, and she looked at him like she wanted to eat him. "Aren't you scrumptious?"

She sat up and traced her cool fingertips along his stomach, following the outlines of his muscles. "Your physique is sinful." Pressing her lips below his navel, she popped the button on his jeans and slid the zipper down.

His senses heightened. He could feel the metal teeth as they disengaged two by two, and as her lips drew nearer to the prize, fire shot through his veins. *Mine,* his owl said in his mind.

Yes. Yes, she would be.

He gripped the hem of her shirt and pulled upward, trying to remove the damn thing, but it wouldn't budge. He tugged at the sides, the front, and the back. "What in Hell's name?"

Lilith laughed. "It was made with magic to protect me. Only I can remove it."

"You don't need protecting from me. I will *never* hurt you." The last part came out like a growl, which was odd. Owls didn't growl, but being here alone with her, exploring each other's bodies, the fated mate bond tightened its hold.

She looked into his eyes. "I know." She moistened her lips before shimmying out of her shirt and tossing her bra aside. "Better?"

"Much." He crawled onto the bed and lay on top of her, taking her mouth in a passionate kiss. The feel of her bare skin pressed to his was almost overwhelming, yet he still felt as if he couldn't get close enough. He needed her. To be inside of her. To be part of her.

He kissed his way down her neck, gliding his lips across her soft, cool skin and flicking out his tongue to bathe her nipple in wet heat. She gasped, and he sucked the pearly flesh into his mouth, cupping the other breast in his hand.

Her breath came out in a hiss as she slid her fingers into his hair. "I've never felt this way about anyone before."

"Neither have I." He trailed his tongue to her belly button, circling it once before continuing to the waistband of her pants. Rising to his knees, he attempted to tug them down, but like her shirt, they were magically glued to her body. "I don't like this fabric."

"I won't wear it again." She wiggled out of the rest of her clothes and lay before him, an ethereal goddess of darkness.

His cock strained against his open zipper, and he yanked down his jeans, tossing his clothes aside before lying on top of her once more. Everything about her was intoxicating. Entrancing.

"My turn." With strength he didn't dare fight, she rolled him onto his back and straddled his thighs. She caressed him with nothing more than her gaze from his eyes down to his dick, and he *felt* it all the way to his bones. When she touched the tip of her tongue to a fang, his cock twitched. Good gravy, he needed her to touch him.

She licked her lips and wrapped her fingers around him. He sucked in a breath and let it out slowly as her soft skin moved against his sensitive flesh. After three more strokes, a bead of moisture gathered on his tip. She spread it over his head with her thumb, and a shudder ran through him, reaching to his soul.

Leaning down, she flicked out her tongue and licked him. Every nerve in his body fired on over-drive, and as she took him into her mouth, he moaned. She stroked the underside of his dick with her tongue as she sucked, bringing him to the brink of orgasm before releasing him.

He panted, trying his damnedest to get himself under control. Lilith was a vixen, unlike any woman he'd ever been with, and no way in hell was he coming before she did.

"I like the way you taste." She kissed each hip before swiping her tongue up his stomach. "Are you ready?"

"Fuck, yes."

Rising onto her knees, she guided him to her folds and sheathed him. She closed her eyes as she took him in fully, tipping her head back and moaning. Spencer sucked in a breath, marveling at her beauty. The feel of her wrapped around him, of becoming one with her, was unlike anything he'd ever felt before.

It was magical.

She opened her eyes and locked her gaze on his, and the tether connecting them tightened even more. Lifting her hips, she slid upward until only his tip remained inside her. She lowered again, the decadent friction making him groan.

He licked his thumb and pressed it to her clit, moving it in gentle circles as she rode him. As her rhythm quickened, he increased the pressure and speed until Lilith cried out in ecstasy. She tightened around him, her body trembling as she panted and moaned.

His orgasm coiled in his core. He couldn't hold out much longer. "Bite me, Lilith. Drink from me."

She lunged forward, wrapping her arms around him and rolling him on top of her, never breaking their intimate union. He leaned his head to the side, giving her full access to his neck as he pumped his hips.

She bit him.

The sharp sting of fangs piercing flesh made him gasp, but as her lips covered the wound and she began to suck, he lost control. The orgasm exploded in his core, lighting his body ablaze. He slammed into her over and over until she let out the most pleasurable groan he'd ever heard. He stilled, holding his hips against her core, and she swiped her tongue over the punctures before wrapping her arms around him and holding him tightly.

Closing his eyes, he buried his face in her hair and just breathed. This was it. His owl was all in, so the man had no choice but to follow. He slipped out of her, rolling onto his back and tugging her to his side. She came to him, resting her head on his chest and draping her leg over his. They lay there in silence, and Lilith became so still, he wondered if she'd fallen asleep.

"That was better than I could have ever imagined," she finally said.

"Yes, it was." He rubbed his palm up and down her arm. He needed to tell her, to know if she felt the same. To understand why fate would bind him with someone who would outlive him for thousands of years. "Why me?"

She propped her head on her hand. "What do you mean?"

"Out of all the men at speed dating… Hell, out of all the men in the world, why did you choose me?"

Her brow furrowed, and her gaze dropped to his chest before returning to his eyes. "Because we're soulmates, Spencer. Fate brought us together."

A flush of cool relief unfurled in his chest, spreading out through his limbs. "You have no idea how happy I am to hear that."

Her smile could have lit the darkest cave in Hell. "You feel it too?"

"I couldn't deny it if I wanted to. My owl has claimed you, but…"

"But I am immortal, and you are not."

"And I don't want to be a vampire." As unbreakable as this bond with Lilith was, he couldn't lose his owl. He couldn't lose half his soul. "What are we going to do?"

"We will figure it out. There must be a way." She tugged on her bottom lip as she thought. "I'm sure Adam still has an in with the being who cursed me. Perhaps I can petition him, beg to be mortal again."

A lump formed in his throat, and his heart wrenched. "You can't give up your immortality for me."

She frowned, sadness filling her eyes. "I suppose not. I haven't spoken to Adam in centuries. I doubt he would help me after the apple debacle anyway."

He pulled her to his chest. "Let's worry about it later. Right now, I just want to be with you."

She snuggled closer. "And be with me you shall."

CHAPTER THIRTEEN

An incessant ringing that sounded like a 1980s telephone dragged Lilith away from a most pleasant dream. She groaned and pulled the blanket over her head like she did every evening when she awoke, but her lids popped open as the most comforting, warm, woodsy scent registered in her senses.

Mmm… Spencer.

Her mouth watered at the memory of his taste. Perhaps it had been her imagination. Deirdre had planted the idea of a cinnamon roll in Lilith's head, but Spencer's blood had sung with notes of spices and copper.

Her stomach tightened, and her lips curved into a smile as the memory danced through her mind. She didn't use an ounce of glamour on him, and his reaction to her raw bite had been orgasmic…for both of them.

The ringing silenced, and she reached for him. He stirred, moving toward her and tugging her to his bare chest. Sweet Persephone, how she loved his warmth. She snuggled against his naked body and closed her eyes.

It was no wonder people raved about this soulmate business. A week ago, Lilith had called the idea bogus. In her mind, the idea of fate creating another person to complete her had sounded preposterous. Yet now, lying here wrapped in Spencer's embrace, complete was the perfect word to describe how she felt. Like a huge part of her soul had been missing all her life because it resided in this beautiful man.

She was finally whole.

She couldn't wait to check in with Deirdre to see how Esther was fairing. If her familiar's fate truly did depend on Lilith finding happiness, the snake was probably slithering all over Deirdre's house, her color and her appetite back to normal.

The ringing ensued again, and this time, it was Spencer who groaned.

"Ignore it." Lilith held him tighter. "I'm not ready for this moment to end."

He pressed his lips to her head and inhaled deeply. "Neither am I, but it's probably Alan."

He leaned over the side of the bed and rummaged through his discarded clothes. "Damnit, Alan. Not a video call." Pushing to a sitting position, he leaned his back against the headboard.

Lilith sat up, holding the blanket to her chest, and Spencer scooted toward her until their bodies touched from their shoulders to their hips and down the length of their legs. "Should I give you some privacy?" she asked as he held the phone out in front of him.

He clutched her thigh with his free hand. "Don't you dare." He hit the button to answer the call. "Hey, man."

"Dude, I've been calling for the past ten minutes. The driver dumped us and our gear outside the gates. He refused to pull all the way in."

"Sorry. I just woke up."

"Damn nocturnals. The sun's setting now. Get your ass out here and help us carry all this stuff in." He squinted, bringing the camera closer to his face. "Lilith?"

Spencer angled his phone toward her, so they were both fully in view.

"Good evening, Alan. Hi, Rebecca." She wiggled her fingers at the camera.

Alan stared, his mouth agape, and Rebecca grinned and said, "This is the part where I say, 'I told you so.'"

Spencer chuckled. "Yeah, you did. Give us a minute to get dressed, and we'll meet you at the gate."

Alan blinked, regaining his composure. "All right. Thanks."

Spencer pressed End and lowered the phone to his lap. "Is it wrong that I wish they'd missed their flight?"

She rested her hand on his chest, and his stomach tensed. "Perhaps, after you get the footage you need, you could come to The Underworld for a bit. I could give you the grand tour, and you could meet Esther."

"I'd like that." He brushed his lips to hers before sliding out of bed. "Where is Percival? I haven't seen him since we flew last night."

She reached out with her mind to connect with her crow and found him pecking at an ear of corn on a nearby farm. *Typical.* "He's out having breakfast."

"I feel bad for locking him out all day." Spencer bent over to retrieve his clothes, and Lilith's stomach fluttered at the sight of his backside. His build was slim yet defined. Not overly muscley, but just toned enough to make her insides burn.

She caught a glimpse of his dick before he pulled on his underwear, and she ran her tongue over her lip at the memory of the way he tasted, how he felt inside her, filling her fully. She would have him again before the night was through and every night for the rest of her existence if she had her way.

"He's fine. Percival appreciates his freedom." She rolled out of bed and dressed, pushing thoughts of all the things she wanted to do with Spencer to the back of her mind for now. They had work to do.

She laced her arm around Spencer's bicep and walked by his side down the stairs. Andrei met them in the foyer, and he inhaled deeply, his brow lifting in surprise. "Can this be?"

Spencer stiffened, and Lilith patted his shoulder. "Can what be, old friend?" she asked.

"The Queen of the Night has found a soulmate in a shifter after all?" He lifted a finger. "Don't try to deny it. I can smell your bond."

"Indeed, I have. Be a dear and help Spencer's friends with their equipment. They are waiting outside the gate."

"Stefan." Andrei waved over one of his human servants. "Take Daniel and retrieve the visitors."

"I better go too." Spencer followed the men out the door, but Lilith hung behind with Andrei.

"How did this happen?" Andrei eyed her, an amused grin curving his lips.

"Speed dating of all things."

"I assume you'll be turning him soon. Or are you still enjoying the taste of his mortal blood?"

Lilith ground her teeth. "He doesn't want to be turned."

"Oh, dear. That is quite the conundrum, isn't it?"

"We'll figure it out. I'm going to help them." She strode out the door and jogged to catch up with Spencer. Thinking about their "conundrum" now would only drag her mind into a dark place. A place she needed to avoid until Esther recovered. Besides, fate wouldn't bless her with this much happiness unless there was a solution to their predicament. She *would* figure out what it was.

Spencer caught her hand, and Percival cawed from a nearby tree. She lifted her free hand, and he swooped down to perch on her fingers. "I trust you had a pleasant day."

He cawed in response and took to the sky once more.

As they reached the gate, Stefan punched in the code to open it. They gathered the gear and returned to the castle to find Andrei standing in the doorway. Rebecca hoisted her camera onto her shoulder, and Alan stopped, turning on his television smile to narrate their journey.

"We finally get to meet the mysterious man whom all the locals believe to be a vampire, Andrei Lupu, the fourth." Alan gestured with his head, and Rebecca panned the scene before focusing on the door.

"I bid you welcome." Andrei bowed formally, and though he spoke perfect English, he thickened his Romanian accent for the show. He'd even donned a regal black cape identical to the one he wore back when Lilith first turned him, and he threw it back with a flourish before turning on his heel and gliding into the castle.

"That was awesome." Rebecca turned off her camera before entering the vampire's home.

Lilith rolled her eyes. Andrei always had a flair for the dramatic, and it seemed it hadn't lessened with time. "You two must be exhausted from travel. Do you want to head up to your rooms and rest, and we can continue tomorrow?" Because the bedroom was exactly where she wanted Spencer.

"Are you kidding?" Alan clasped his hands behind his back and peered at one of Andrei's old suits of armor. "I'm way too wired to sleep. Are you up for an interview, Mr. Lupu?"

"Always. And please, call me Andrei." He gestured to a doorway. "You may set up your cameras in my library."

"Well, I wouldn't mind brushing my teeth," Rebecca said. "Can you rein in your excitement for half an hour, Bigfoot?"

"I, too, would like a quick shower." Lilith winked at Spencer, and an adorable blush rose on his cheeks. "Meet in the library in thirty?"

"Very well." Andrei bowed. "Stefan will show you to your rooms."

They followed Stefan to their wing, but before Alan stepped into his room, he gave Spencer a hard look. "Thirty minutes."

Spencer simply chuckled and opened his door.

Lilith waited for Rebecca to disappear into her own chamber before following Spencer into his. He raked his gaze down her body and clutched her hips, pulling them flush against his and taking her mouth in a tender kiss. The fine hairs on her arms stood at attention as warm shivers cascaded through her body. She leaned into him, wrapping her arms around his shoulders and deepening the kiss.

"You should have asked for more than thirty minutes," he whispered against her lips.

"I'm sure they won't mind if we're a little late."

He laughed and pressed his forehead to hers. "Alan will most definitely mind. He's a stickler with schedules."

"I guess we'll have to shower together then." She ran a finger down his chest, stopping at the waistband of his jeans. "Get clean while we're being dirty."

"With all the things I'd want to do to you, there's no way we'd be done in half an hour. Let's wait until the others go to sleep."

She pouted her lower lip. "You, sir, are no fun at all."

"I promise I'll make the wait worth your while."

"Oh, fine." She grinned and headed for the hallway. "I will hold you to that promise."

"I hope you do." His seductive smile made her spine tingle.

A text pinged her phone, Deirdre's name lighting up the screen, and she swiped it open. The text contained a picture of Esther curled on the couch next to Azrael's cat, Tabitha. Her color had returned, thankfully, and the message read: *Keep doing what you're doing. Esther is recovering.*

"You mean keep doing *whom* I'm doing." She

snickered and closed her door before typing a quick reply: *Sending her my love. Thank you for the update.*

Lilith showered—sadly, alone—at vampire speed and applied a light coat of makeup before slipping back inside Spencer's room at the most opportune time. He stepped out of the ensuite bathroom naked, his skin pink from the heat of the shower. His pheromones flared when he glimpsed her sitting on the bed, the most alluring fragrance of spices and home.

He chuckled and grabbed a pair of boxer briefs from his bag. "Couldn't wait, huh?"

"I wanted a sneak peek of the promises that await."

He held out his arms and turned in a circle. "All this can be yours for the small price of a little patience."

"Patience has never been one of my virtues, but I will try my best." Watching the man perform the simple act of getting dressed made a chocolate fountain bubble in her core, the gooey warm goodness spreading through her body, delighting her in a way she'd never experienced before.

They met the others in the library, and Lilith sat in a cigar chair next to Andrei as they set up their equipment. Rebecca positioned a strange, rectangular light covered in white fabric to shine on Andrei, and Spencer attached his camera to a tripod.

"Do you mind if I take that seat?" Alan asked.

"Of course." Lilith moved to a small couch adjacent to the chairs and crossed her legs, clasping her hands on her knee. Spencer counted backward from five on his fingers, pointed at Alan, and the show began.

"Greetings, fellow cryptid hunters. I'm in the castle of the village's resident vampire, Andrei Lupu, the fourth. Tell me, Andrei, what makes the people of this small town believe you're a creature of the night?"

"My family has lived in this castle for hundreds of years. I bear a strong resemblance to my dearly departed father, Andrei Lupu, the third, and he to his father." Andrei steepled his fingers as he spun the tale. He had explained to the village elders, many times over, that he was simply a descendent of the original owner. He even convinced them one of his servant's sons was his own. Still, the rumor...the truth... spread through the village like a fable parents told small children to make them stay in their beds at night.

"My son, Andrei Lupu, the fifth, will one day be the man of this castle, and I am certain he will be accused of being a vampire, as I and my father and grandfather were."

"So the rumors of bloodletting, of virgins being sacrificed in blood orgies, of townsfolk venturing too close to the castle and disappearing…? All untrue?"

"Nothing more than gossip. Ask Lilith. She has stayed in my castle on several occasions. Did we sacrifice any virgins that you are aware of?" Andrei gestured, and Spencer panned the camera toward her.

Lilith gave her head a tiny shake and smiled. "Andrei has been accused of many things. He's a brute, a snob, and he tells horrible jokes that no one finds funny. But a murderer, he is not."

Of course, she wasn't certain about the murderer part. Killing villagers wasn't in Andrei's best interest, but Lilith was the mother of vampires, not the queen. How they governed themselves was up to them. If she'd known her children would have the power to create more vampires, she might not have turned the dozen or so she did in the beginning, but what happened happened. No sense in dwelling on the past, especially not when her future was grinning at her from behind a camera.

Alan spoke, and Spencer turned the lens back to him. "So far, Andrei's bloodline has been spared the stake, but others haven't been so lucky. I hear the oldest cemetery in Romania lies on your property and that the people buried there were done so with an interesting ritual."

Andrei nodded. "The belief in vampires runs backward for hundreds of years. Many plagues have swept through the land that caused unexplainable bleeding from the orifices, jaundice, agitation, and a plethora of other symptoms. Medicine being what it was, the only explanations that made sense to the people of the time were supernatural."

"What happened when these people died?"

"The villagers feared death was not the end for these sufferers, and they staked them to the ground when they buried them, believing the corpse would not reanimate if it couldn't leave its grave."

"So if we were to dig up one of these graves, we'd find a skeleton with a stake through his heart?"

"The heart, the stomach, the throat, and you wouldn't be the first person to uncover the deceased. People frequently dug up the graves of their loved ones to check for signs of vampirism. Unfortunately, ignorance about the way corpses decay caused even more panic…and more staking of the dead."

Alan rested his elbow on the arm of the chair, leaning toward Andrei. "Is this still in practice today?"

"Not in my cemetery. This is private property, and I do not allow it."

"Would you be willing to let us excavate one, so the people at home can learn about this ancient tradition?"

Andrei inhaled deeply, as if contemplating the question, even though he'd already agreed. "In the name of education, yes. I will permit your team to disturb a single grave, as long as it is recovered and left as you found it."

Alan grinned at the camera. "Get ready, folks. We're going to find ourselves a vampire."

CHAPTER FOURTEEN

At the conclusion of the interview, Andrei rose from his chair. "I did not anticipate your enthusiasm, and I planned a feast for this evening. If you are in a hurry to complete your filming, I can postpone it."

Spencer's stomach growled. "I could eat."

Rebecca scrunched her face. "By feast, I hope you mean food for your guests and not your guests as food."

Amusement danced in Andrei's eyes. "I'm sure Lilith has already sampled one of you." He looked at Spencer, and everyone followed his gaze.

Spencer swallowed hard. What could he say? It was true, but that didn't mean his friends should be on the menu.

Andrei chuckled. "As host, it's only fair if I…"

Spencer eyed him warily, trying to discern if the old vampire was serious, and Lilith moved to his side.

"Whoa, man." Alan raised his hands. "Nobody's fangs are getting anywhere near my neck."

"Any vein will do." Andrei smirked.

Spencer's feathers ruffled beneath his skin, and Lilith patted his shoulder reassuringly. "That's enough, Andrei." She looked at Alan. "Do you see what I mean about his jokes not being funny?"

Alan let out a nervous laugh. "Yeah."

Andrei smiled, showing fang. "Of course I mean a feast for my guests. It has been ages since the cook has prepared food for the formal dining room, and she is quite excited to exercise her skills."

"And we aren't on the menu?" Rebecca asked.

Andrei swept his gaze down her body before meeting her eyes. "Not unless you want to be, *iubi*."

She blushed and cleared her throat. "*Iubi?*"

"It's Romanian for darling."

"Andrei, you are impossible." Lilith gestured toward the dining room. "I assure you all that no vampire here will drink from you. You are perfectly safe."

He grinned at Rebecca. "Indeed, you are, my friends. Come. Let us feast."

Spencer walked by Lilith's side into the biggest dining room he'd ever seen. Seriously, the place was as big as his entire apartment, and a long mahogany table stretched down the center. Eighteen chairs lined the massive hunk of wood, with place settings for five at the far end.

Andrei took a seat at the head of the table, and Lilith sat next to Spencer, with Alan and Rebecca across from them. Two servants scurried in to fill their glasses with red wine, though Andrei and Lilith's "wine" looked more like blood.

Another set of servants brought plates covered with silver domes, and they set them in front of everyone, including the vampires.

Rebecca cocked her head. "You eat food? I thought you only drank blood."

"I enjoy a rare steak every now and then," Lilith said.

"You're all predator shifters, so I trust none of you are vegetarians," Andrei said, and the servants removed the domes, revealing massive sides of beef and piles of potatoes.

Spencer's mouth watered until he glanced at Lilith's plate. Her meat was so rare, it looked raw, and as she cut into it, blood oozed onto her plate. His abdomen clenched, and he expected his stomach to roil. But as she parted her red lips and brought the fork to her mouth, his own blood rushed to his groin.

Strange. The sight of blood had never nauseated him, but it also had *never* turned him on. Then again, he'd never been head over tail feathers for a vampire before either.

Lilith swallowed the steak and rested her hand on his thigh, breaking the mini trance he'd succumbed to. He glanced at his friends, who were chowing down on their meals, and he picked up his fork.

The meat was medium rare, savory, and so tender it practically melted on his tongue. The potatoes tasted of cream and black pepper, and before he knew it, he was scraping the final forkful from his plate.

Alan wiped his mouth with a napkin and dropped it onto the table. "That was an amazing meal, Andrei. Thanks."

"Delicious," Rebecca added.

"Best meal I've had in a long time," Spencer said.

Lilith tightened her grip on his thigh. "Perhaps we should turn in for the night and get a fresh start tomorrow."

Spencer placed his hand on hers and squeezed. He couldn't wait to get her alone.

"Are you kidding?" Alan said as the servants cleared their plates. "It's only nine o'clock, and my adrenaline is peaking. Let's uncover the corpse tonight, and then you love birds can have all the alone time you want." He rose to his feet.

"I wouldn't mind doing the hard part now." Rebecca stood next to Alan. "Then we can relax tomorrow. Maybe Andrei can give us a tour of the castle?"

"It would be my pleasure." Andrei stood and gestured toward the foyer.

Spencer let out a slow breath. When Alan got this excited, he wouldn't take no for an answer. If he wanted any peace on this excursion, it was best to give in and get it over with. "All right. Let's do it."

They gathered their gear and headed toward the back of the castle.

"I should warn you." Andrei stopped at the door as Spencer and his team stepped onto the portico. "Real vampires are also buried in the cemetery as well. Be respectful when unearthing the grave."

"But they're staked, so they're dead, right?" Spencer adjusted his gear bag on his shoulder.

Andrei cast Lilith a sideways glance and spread his hands as if to say, "Obviously." At least, that was how

Spencer took it. He still wasn't sure what to make of this guy, but at least he didn't feel the churn of jealousy about their past relationship anymore. Not now that he knew how Lilith felt about him.

He still had a hard time wrapping his mind around how a woman of power and notoriety like Lilith—a woman who could have any man she wanted—had chosen a man like him. His owl had no trouble believing it, of course. He was determined to make Lilith his mate, and Spencer knew better than to ignore his owl's instincts.

The last time he ignored his bird was five years ago. It had been days since he'd hunted, and his owl was starving, but he ignored his avian instinct to hunt and spent the night with his human girlfriend instead. His owl had taken over in his sleep, shifted right there in the bed, and devoured her pet ferret. *Whoops.*

On the plus side, his girlfriend had slept through the entire ordeal, and he'd convinced her the animal had escaped through an open window. He'd learned his lesson, though. His owl wanted Lilith, and he would do his damnedest to figure out a way to make it happen.

A nagging little voice in the back of his mind

tried to remind him how he'd let a powerful woman destroy him before, but he squelched it. Lilith was different. She was his fated mate; she would never hurt him.

"Through the garden and take a left before the maze," Andrei said. "The cemetery lies half a mile to the east."

"You won't be joining us?" Lilith asked.

"I would rather have my fangs pulled than watch an undead brother be unearthed."

"Thanks again for letting us do this." Spencer shook Andrei's hand before wrapping an arm around Lilith's waist. "Let's get this footage down before the sun comes up."

He took the lead, with Lilith by his side, and the four of them ventured into the garden. Moonlight cast a silvery glow over the topiaries, and Percival cawed from somewhere in the distance, bringing a smile to Spencer's lips.

"Have you heard how Esther is doing?" he asked.

"She seems to be making a full recovery, thanks to you."

"I'm glad I could help. When we get back, I'd love to meet her."

Lilith grinned. "She will be thrilled to meet you. This is where we make a left." She pointed ahead to the topiary maze. A wall of neatly trimmed hedges towering seven feet high blocked their path, and a six-foot arch cut into the bush provided entrance into the labyrinth.

"Do you think Andrei would let us go in the maze tomorrow?" Rebecca ran her hand over the wall. "I've always wanted to conquer one of these."

Spencer shook his head. "No, thank you. I've seen *The Shining*. No way I'm getting lost in that thing."

"Pfft." Rebecca waved a hand dismissively. "You can't get lost. You can fly out."

They hung a left and headed toward the cemetery.

"I'm down," Alan said. "We can shoot some footage inside."

"Feel free to ask him." Lilith clutched Spencer's bicep. "We nocturnals will be spending the day in bed…I mean, indoors."

Spencer's stomach tightened. In bed, in the shower, bent over the bathroom counter. He didn't care where they were as long as Lilith was naked and in his arms.

"Not all day." Alan wagged a finger at them. "We have to go into town to interview the believers. This adventure is coming together fantastically. Andrei is great on camera. You are too, Lilith. Want to help me dig?"

She held up the shovel she carried. "What do you think I brought this for?"

The crew chatted on the half-mile trek to the graveyard, Lilith fitting in with his friends as if she'd been part of the team all along. They stopped when their destination came into view, and Spencer set up his camera, hoisting it onto his shoulder to film their arrival. Rebecca set down her bag and prepared her camera, while Alan held a shovel and gestured for Lilith to join him in front of the lenses.

"We've arrived at Lupu Cemetery," Alan said, "on the private property of Andrei Lupu, the fourth. He's given us special permission to unearth a grave so the world can see the strange burial rituals practiced hundreds of years ago, up until this day."

Spencer followed as he and Lilith walked toward the entrance. A four-foot wrought-iron fence enclosed the small cemetery, and the gate hung askew on its hinges. It creaked in horror movie fashion when Alan opened it, and Spencer's pulse raced. Rebecca panned her camera across the graves, the dilapidated headstones sinking into the earth at odd angles, exactly the way one would imagine in a haunted graveyard. Viewers would be on the edges of their seats as they watched this episode.

"My friend Lilith is an expert in vampire lore, and

she's here to help me with the excavation." Alan rested a hand on Lilith's shoulder, and Spencer held in a chuckle. An expert in vampire lore. That was an understatement.

Spencer paused the recording. "You look great on camera, Lilith." His compliment earned him a smile, and he stepped past them, entering the cemetery first and turning his lens on them once more.

"Andrei didn't specify which grave we should excavate," Alan said into the camera before turning to Lilith. "Do you have a preference?"

She pursed her lips and cast her gaze across their choices. "That one looks promising."

Spencer turned to the grave in question. A pile of rounded stones covered the earth, but no headstone marked the burial site.

Alan chuckled. "Of course you pick the one that will take the most work to uncover."

"Whomever this person was, the living wanted to make damn sure he didn't escape his grave." She pressed her fingers to her lips. "Oops. I shouldn't say that on camera, should I? Do I need to say it again without the curse word?"

Spencer paused his camera. "It's fine. Alan drops a few F-bombs every now and then. The editors will bleep it out."

Rebecca set up a floodlight on the grave, and Spencer filmed Alan and Lilith removing the first few stones before setting down his camera and helping them with the rest. With the stones set aside, he resumed filming as they dug up the shallow grave.

Percival flew into the frame and landed at the edge of the hole. He cawed and hopped toward Lilith, but she kept in character and tried to appear human. She waved an arm and said, "Shoo."

The crow screeched at her, ruffling his feathers before flying directly at the camera. He angled upward inches from the lens, circled over Spencer's head, and landed on his shoulder before letting out a caw so close to the microphone that it was sure to give the viewers a good jump scare. The network execs were going to eat this episode up.

"I see bones." Alan dropped his shovel and kneeled beside the hole. Lilith joined him, and they continued digging with their hands. Spencer moved in close while Rebecca filmed a wider shot.

"Here's his head." Lilith cupped her hands around a mummified skull. "Do you have brushes to remove the dirt?"

"Yeah." Alan retrieved two brushes from a duffel bag, and they gently removed the earth covering the corpse.

Spencer zoomed in on the remains, and Alan and Lilith backed away so he could get a clear shot. He'd expected to find nothing more than a skeleton and a few splinters from the wooden stake they'd used in the burial. This body, however, was fully intact, though emaciated.

The sickly greenish-brown skin stretched taut over bones, and the eye sockets had sunken in like all the viscous matter in the eyeballs had long since evaporated. Spindly arms crossed the man's chest, and his ragged clothing looked frail enough to disintegrate if it were moved.

The stake pinning the man to the ground wasn't wooden, nor did it pierce the heart. A rusted iron rod penetrated the corpse through the upper abdomen instead.

"Staking the heart wasn't widely common when this man died," Lilith explained, and Spencer turned the camera toward her. "With many diseases rendering people catatonic, being buried alive was sadly quite common."

"And with burials this shallow," Alan said. "I imagine they experienced a few people rising from the grave."

Lilith nodded solemnly. "The stake was meant to keep them in the ground."

"Looks like it worked for this poor fellow," Alan said. "Should we remove it? Let him finally rest in peace?"

"Andrei requested we leave the graves as we found them." Sadness filled Lilith's eyes, and Spencer's gut wrenched. She was responsible for the vampire population. He couldn't imagine how she felt seeing someone treated this way.

She sniffed and straightened her spine, regaining her composure. "Villages like this one still do not practice embalming on the dead, so it's not uncommon for the deceased to be buried with stakes through their hearts today."

"Fascinating," Alan said before making a cutting motion across his throat.

Spencer lowered his camera and turned his back to the grave to wave over Rebecca. She jogged toward him and froze, her gaze glued to the ground in front of him.

The hissing registered in his senses first. He glanced down, and his muscles seized. Six inches from his ankle lay a horned viper, coiled and poised to strike. Gods, how he hated snakes. His owl rose to the surface, but before his fight or flight instinct brought on the shift, he stumbled backward into the grave.

The snake struck, its fangs piercing his jeans and

sinking into his flesh. His leg kicked out instinctively, knocking the iron stake from the ground and sending the snake flying across the grave. Spencer's ass met the dirt, and he clutched his ankle. The bite stung like a thousand fire ants had crawled through the punctures and were making their way upward toward his heart.

"Spencer!" Lilith darted toward him, and everything around him seemed to move in slow motion. She kneeled by his side, first taking his face in her hands, and then turning toward the corpse, her eyes growing wide as it sat upright in its grave.

Its head slowly turned toward Alan, and dust and clumps of hair rained down around its shoulders. Its bones creaked with the movement as if they were living in a horror movie.

Alan peered at the living corpse, an expression of awe making him look ten years younger. His mouth hung open, his eyes blinking rapidly.

It lunged.

"No!" Lilith shot from Spencer's side, leaping over the grave and tackling the *still* undead vampire. They rolled over each other, the corpse stopping on top of her and landing a punch to her jaw before leaping to its feet.

Spencer sat on the ground, stunned and in agony. He should have shifted. He should have gotten the hell out of the way, but he just sat there as the vampire corpse barreled toward him and latched onto his neck. He vaguely heard the sounds of Lilith's screams and Alan's sasquatch grunt before the vampire gnashed down and ripped out his carotid artery.

CHAPTER FIFTEEN

L ilith let out a guttural roar that shook the pits of Hell. She leaped to her feet and charged the blood-lusting vampire. Wrapping her arms around the vile fiend's waist, she ripped him from Spencer's body, tumbling over and over as the creature lashed and screamed.

She landed next to the metal stake, and she threw the vampire off her before clutching the rod and marching toward it. It hissed, baring its fangs, and Percival swooped down, pecking at its eyes before she plunged the hunk of metal into its heart, pinning it to the ground.

It flailed its arms and legs a final time before Lilith ripped off its head, ending its undead life for good.

"Lilith! Lilith, you have to help him!" Rebecca sat next to Spencer, her hands pressed against his neck, blood oozing between her fingers.

"Come on, buddy. Stay with us." Alan rested one hand on Spencer's chest and patted his cheek with the other.

"Let me see the wound." Lilith dropped to her knees.

Rebecca removed her hands, and blood spurted from Spencer's neck in time with his decelerating heart. Lilith covered the gash, applying pressure to slow the bleeding, but he'd lost so much blood already. There was no way he would survive.

Her heart wrenched in her chest, and tears streamed down her cheeks as his life force seeped between her fingers. This was her fault. Once again, her brilliant plan ended in disaster, and this time, Spencer paid the price.

An agonizing ache clenched in her stomach, spiraling up to her throat, thickening it until she couldn't speak, couldn't breathe. Fate had to know this would happen. That Lilith would destroy the one good thing in her life because everything she touched turned to ruin.

Fate was a cruel bitch. And Lilith…

She'd been selfish. Her immortality had made her

careless. She knew the dangers of awakening a vampire who hadn't been staked properly, but she hadn't stopped to think about the consequences of unearthing one.

Closing her eyes, she swallowed the lump of hot coal from her throat, but another one lodged in its place. A piece of her soul resided in Spencer, and when he died, he would take it with him. She would never recover. She could not live without him.

Spencer coughed, and blood spewed from his lips before he stilled. Lilith removed her hands from the wound. His heart ceased to beat. The world stopped turning.

"Damnit, Lilith. Turn him!" Alan shouted.

Lilith didn't dare move. If she did, she would fall apart.

Rebecca put a firm hand on her shoulder. "You have to turn him."

She forced a whisper from her raw throat. "He doesn't want to be turned."

"He'd rather be undead than really dead." Alan stood and raked a hand through his hair. "You can't let him die."

"I cannot turn him into a creature he would detest." She loved him too much to disregard his wishes, yet... Gazing into his unblinking eyes, she wiped the tears from her cheeks. She also loved him too much to let him go.

"He doesn't detest you." Tears welled in Alan's eyes, making Lilith's fall faster. He huffed, shaking his head as if he couldn't believe her.

Rebecca moved to Spencer's other side, looking Lilith in the eyes. "You've changed his mind about vampires, and I know you don't want to live without him. Given the choice between being dead and being a vampire, he'd choose to be with you."

Lilith nodded. "He would forgive me." They were soulmates. How could he not?

"There'd be nothing to forgive. You have the power to save his life. Use it."

The air shimmered next to her, the energy condensing and expanding until it pricked at her skin. *No. This can't be happening.*

"What the hell?" Alan cocked his head, drawing his brow downward, and Azrael appeared before them, his wicked scythe clutched in both his hands.

"The Angel of Death." Rebecca's voice was barely a whisper.

Lilith ground her teeth, her face pinching as rage extinguished the sadness inside her. Rising to her knees, she leaned over Spencer protectively. "How dare you? I won't let you take him."

Azrael gave her a sympathetic look. "I don't choose who lives or dies. Fate has decided it's his time."

"No! You can't have him." Her mind blanked, instinct taking over, and she plunged her fangs into Spencer's shoulder. She took a single sip of his blood, just enough to form a magical connection, before biting her wrist and pressing it to his mouth.

"Drink, sweetheart, and we can be together forever." She brushed the hair from his forehead and pressed a kiss to his clammy skin.

He didn't move, didn't accept her offering of eternal life, so she tugged on his chin with her thumb, parting his lips. Her blood dripped onto his tongue, slowly filling his mouth with her gift.

"Swallow, please. One little gulp is all it will take."

Azrael lingered beside her, a solemn expression drawing his features down. Was she too late? Had her hesitation doomed the man she loved to the afterlife? *Why the fuck can't I do anything right?* "Please, Spencer. I need you in my life. I love you."

His lids fluttered, and he swallowed her blood.

The heavy weight in her chest dropped into her stomach before disintegrating into relief. Fresh tears gathered on her lower lids, spilling down her cheeks, and an ill-timed laugh bubbled up from somewhere deep inside her.

"That's it." She pressed her wrist harder against his lips. "Take some more. You've got a massive wound to heal." She looked up at Azrael, who nodded once and disappeared.

Spencer's eyes flew open, the deep brown of his irises holding her hostage as he drank from her vein. Her stomach fluttered, and warmth spread through her core at the intensity of his gaze. She would have let him drain her dry if that was what it would take to save his life, but his wound was already on the mend.

Gently, she pulled her wrist from his grasp. "That's enough, my love. My blood is powerful; we don't want to overwhelm your system."

Spencer closed his eyes and let out a sigh. Whether it was from contentment, relief, or fatigue, it didn't matter. He was healing. But she had turned him into a creature of the night. Her curse was now his burden.

She sat back on her heels, watching as the sleep of death pulled him under, beginning the transformation. Nausea churned in her gut, and she bit her bottom lip, the sharp sting of her fangs pressing into her flesh keeping her grounded.

"Is that it?" Rebecca asked. "He'll be okay now?"

Good question. That was still to be determined. "I'm not sure I've done the right thing."

"You saved his life."

"And turned him into a creature he specifically stated he did not want to become. He just told me a second time a few hours ago." Had she been selfish yet again? *Gah!* She'd never been so indecisive in her life.

"That was when he had a choice." Rebecca moved to Lilith's side and rested a hand on her shoulder. "You did the right thing. You'll see."

"What happens now?" Alan asked.

She looked at Spencer, wiping the blood from his lips with her thumb. "He will sleep for three days, possibly more. His wound was deep, and it may slow the transformation."

"And this thing…?" He toed the corpse with his shoe. "It's really dead now?"

"Yes, he is finally at peace."

Rebecca's face pinched. "Was he alive the whole time he was in the grave?"

"Undead and starving. His bloodlust was uncontrollable, and…" She sucked in a shaky breath. "I'm so sorry. I put all of you at risk."

"Nobody forced us to come here," Alan said.

"And anyway, the footage we have is going to save us. You saved our show; I know it."

Lilith nodded. Hopefully some good would come of this. "I need to take him inside before sunrise. I will clean him up, and if you don't mind, I would like to take him to The Underworld. Being in The Underworld will help with the transformation."

"Of course." Rebecca rose to her feet. "Whatever you need to do. We can rebury the corpse and bring in the equipment, right Alan?"

"Yeah. Just take care of our boy. We all need him in our lives."

"I will do my best." Lilith scooped Spencer's lifeless body into her arms and carried him to the castle.

CHAPTER SIXTEEN

Lilith brought Spencer to her home in The Underworld, and three days came and went while she never left his side. Deirdre had stopped by the first day to return Esther, but other than that, Lilith hadn't seen a single soul. Percival took daily flights around The Underworld, but she didn't bother connecting with him. She didn't want to speak to anyone. Not while Spencer lay in limbo.

Esther had nearly made a full recovery. Dee told her the snake had been on death's door for a moment, and she didn't mean Azrael's front porch. No doubt when Spencer lay dying, her familiar could barely withstand the agony tearing Lilith apart. She would have lost them both if she hadn't turned Spencer. She had done the right thing.

She had done the right thing.

Hadn't she?

Esther's color had returned, she was eating, and she spent her time wrapped around Lilith's shoulders or coiled on Spencer's stomach. She'd taken to Spencer the moment she saw him, as she should have. He was her soulmate too.

She had done the right thing. So, why was her stomach still tied in knots?

"Lilith?" Eve's voice sounded from the living room. "I know you said no visitors, but we came to check on you anyway. Is he awake yet?"

"Not yet." Reluctantly, she rose from her seat beside the bed and padded down the hall. "Come back here. I don't want to leave him alone."

"We don't want to disturb him," Venus said.

Deirdre motioned for them to follow her to the bedroom. "Believe me. He's dead to the world right now. He won't hear a thing."

The women filed into the room and stood around the bed. "He's a cutie pie, isn't he?" Eve said.

Dee smiled at him. "Adorable."

"And a sweetheart too," Venus said.

Lilith cringed. "We'll see how sweet he wants to be when he wakes up and realizes what I've done. I'm afraid he'll hate me."

"Why would he hate you?" the Goddess of Love asked.

"Because he made it quite clear he did not want to be a vampire. What if I've done the wrong thing by turning him?"

"Pfft." Deirdre waved a hand dismissively. "He'll get over that real quick."

"How do you know? Were you turned against your will?"

"Well, no, but my sire abandoned me a few years later, and I got over it."

Lilith crossed her arms. "And how long did that take?"

Dee shrugged. "Just a century or so."

Lilith sighed and sank onto the edge of the bed. "Fangtastic. He's going to hate me for a century."

"No, he won't." Eve patted her shoulder. "You're not going to abandon him. That's the difference."

"Never. I love him."

"Everything will work out," Venus said. "Ladies, let's give Lilith some privacy. You know where to find us if you need anything."

Lilith nodded. "Thank you."

Her friends left, and Lilith gazed at her soulmate lying on the bed. Esther had taken her favorite spot on Spencer's belly, and Lilith lay beside them in the bed while Percival sat between them. She never realized how much of her heart resided outside her body until this moment. She'd taken her familiars for granted, assumed they would always be with her. She knew now that she had to take care of them and of herself.

Spencer's eyes moved beneath his lids, and Lilith sat up, her muscles tensing. She would never take this man for granted, and she would show him every day for the rest of eternity how much of her heart resided in him.

Percival rose to his feet, watching the movement intently, and a light flush of color returned to Spencer's ashen cheeks. Though he didn't need to breathe, he sucked in a gasp of air, and his eyes opened.

Spencer lay still, staring at the ceiling in a dark room. A weight lay on his stomach, and something or someone stirred beside him. His throat felt like he'd swallowed an electric sander—while it was running— and his mouth tasted of copper, but otherwise, he felt okay. A little foggy, but no worse for wear.

The ceiling above didn't look like anything he'd

seen before. Painted black, it had millions of tiny crystals scattered across it like stars. Where the hell was he?

Think, Spence. Think. What's the last thing you remember?

The cavern in the rainforest had been covered with crystals like this. Had the cave-in knocked him out? Had the past few weeks been nothing more than a dream? No, that wasn't possible. He'd found his soulmate; he hadn't imagined that. Speed dating… Costa Rica…

Romania. He and Lilith had spent the night at Andrei's castle, and Alan and Rebecca met them there the next day. Then what? He squeezed his eyes shut, trying to chase the fog from his mind. They interviewed Andrei. Or…they were going to interview him. Had they done it?

Yes, the memory was vague, but he recalled the library and how good Lilith looked on camera. Then they'd gone to the cemetery, and… No, that part had to be a nightmare.

"Spencer?" Lilith's fingers brushed his forehead, and he opened his eyes to find her gazing at him lovingly.

Relief washed over him. "I had the wildest dream." He rose onto his elbows, and his gaze locked on the thing weighing down his stomach…a snake.

A fucking snake.

"Ahh!" Without thinking, without assessing what kind of snake it might be, whether or not its bite could kill him, or even *why* it was lying on his stomach, he grabbed it behind its head and flung it across the room.

His fight or flight kicked in, and he shot to his feet, ready for his owl to take over. He shifted his weight, preparing to take flight, but he froze. Something was wrong. Very, very wrong. Feathers didn't prick beneath his skin. Magic didn't hum through his bones. He stood there, and…nothing happened.

"Esther!" Lilith paced toward the snake and picked it up while Spencer squeezed his eyes shut, focusing on his inner owl and willing it to the surface.

It wasn't there.

He clutched his chest before raking his fingers through his hair, pulling it at the roots. "What the fuck is happening?"

He felt hollow, like a piece of him had been ripped from his psyche and shredded into a million particles before being cast to the wind. "Lilith?"

She clutched the snake in her hands, and it coiled around her arm, flicking out its forked tongue. "It's okay, my pet. Spencer was stunned. He didn't mean to hurt you."

"Your pet?"

"This is Esther, my familiar that you helped save."

All this time, she'd been trying to save a fucking snake? He shook his head. He couldn't think about it now. Right now, the only important thing was his owl. "What happened? Why can't I shift?"

She put the snake in a terrarium and turned on a heat lamp. "It's important that your animal be neutralized during the transformation. How do you feel? Oh, you must be parched. It's been ages since I've done this. Come." She motioned for him to follow and strode down the hallway.

"Neutralized during the…" His stomach sank down to his shoes. *Oh, hell no.* She wouldn't. This couldn't… His hands trembled as he slowly reached toward his mouth and ran his fingers over his teeth.

Fangs.

She'd turned him into a fucking vampire.

His owl was dead.

"What the fuck have you done to me?" He marched down the hall and found her in the kitchen, pouring a thick red liquid into a glass.

She pursed her lips. "You're hangry. Let's get some

blood in you, and your emotions will settle." She offered him the glass.

The scent wafted to his senses, making his mouth water and his head spin. Rich and luscious, it had hints of nutmeg and vanilla, like the cookies his grandma used to bake. But it was *blood*. He crossed his arms. No way in Lucifer's realm was he drinking that.

She held it toward him for a moment before setting it on the counter and flashing a hesitant smile. "You need to drink—"

"I don't want it. I don't want *this*." He flung his hands in the air. "You killed my owl, Lilith." He snapped her name with enough venom to paralyze a cow, making her flinch. "How could you? I told you I didn't want this."

"I didn't kill your owl; I saved your life. Do you not remember?"

He didn't know whether to scream or cry. A deep, agonizing ache wrenched in his chest, and the heat of anger burning in his veins made his fists clench. "Do I not remember a zombie vampire ripping my throat out? Yeah, I remember. I also remember telling you multiple times that I did not want to be turned."

"You would have died otherwise."

"You should have let me. Death would be better than this."

Her lips parted, and tears gathered on her lower lids. "Your friends begged me to."

"And what they want is more important than what I want?"

She lowered her head, gazing at the counter and drumming her fingers. When she looked up at him, a single tear slid down her cheek. "I love you, Spencer. I couldn't live without you."

No. He couldn't bear to hear those words from her. Not now. Not when she'd killed half his soul to keep him alive forever. An eternity without his owl…

A flash of anger burned white-hot in his chest. "You did it on purpose. You set the whole thing up so you'd have an excuse to turn me without my consent."

She gaped. "What are you talking about?"

"Traveling to Romania, digging up the body. You knew that vampire would still be alive when we unearthed it; that's why you chose that grave. You planted the snake because you know how much I hate them." He knew as the words tumbled from his lips that they weren't true. He didn't believe what he was saying, but he couldn't stop the venomous accusations from spilling. "You did it all so you could keep me forever." He gestured to Percival, who stood on the back of a chair. "So I could be one of your pets."

Her nostrils flared as she let out a slow breath. "I saved your life."

"You shouldn't have. I can't live without my owl."

"Your owl—"

He held up a hand. "Save it. I have to get out of here."

"Spencer, wait. This is the hunger talking. Your system isn't functioning properly because you need blood." She pushed the glass toward him. "Please drink."

"No. Leave me alone. I can't even look at you right now." He strode for the door, slamming it behind him harder than he'd planned, but fuck it. His very being had been altered. He was allowed to act pissy.

He paced through Lilith's front yard, past her flower garden, filled with colorful daisies and lilacs, and stepped through the picket fence onto the side-walk. A silver moon hung against a midnight back-drop, with sparkling stars splayed all around, but it couldn't be real. They were in the bowels of The Underworld; there was no sky in Hell.

The Underworld looked nothing like he'd imag-ined, and if he were in a better mindset, he might have stopped to take it all in. Instead, he wandered up and down the streets, barely making eye contact with the people he passed. He had no idea where he was going or how to get back to Lilith's, but he didn't care. The walls of his throat seemed to be melded together, and every time he swallowed, it felt like the flesh was being ripped apart.

Well, what now, Spence? He found a stone bench at the entrance to a small park, and he sank onto it, holding his pounding head in his hands. A sob bubbled up from deep in his chest, and he squeezed his eyes shut, willing the tears to stay in his body where they belonged. An image of Lilith's crumpled expression as he spewed his toxic words at her appeared in his mind. The hurt in her eyes had been palpable. She really thought she'd done him a favor by turning him.

And, hell, maybe she had. Maybe… But his owl… A fist of pain clenched in his stomach, making him double over. His head throbbed, and his throat was officially sealed shut. He couldn't swallow, and the simple act of breathing felt like he was sucking in fire.

Oh, wait. He didn't have to breathe anymore because he was dead. No better than the corpse that ripped out his throat.

He groaned. That wasn't true. Lilith had been a vampire for millennia, and she felt plenty alive to him. He pictured her face again and added heartache to the plethora of pain. He'd been an ass. No one deserved to be spoken to like that, especially not his fated mate.

But without his owl, had his fate changed? Would he even feel the same intense connection to her? *Fuck.* Right now, all he felt was anguish.

"Spencer? Is that you, hon?" A woman sat beside him, and he glanced at her through slitted eyes. Venus.

"Where's Lilith?" A vampire with long, brown hair sat on his other side.

"She killed my owl." The words felt like razor blades in his throat.

The vampire typed something on her phone and let out a long sigh. "Come on. Up you go." She grabbed his arm and tugged him to his feet. "You're coming to The Fang and Flask."

"Eve, dear, care to fill me in?" Venus snaked her arm around his bicep, helping to move him along. "I read hearts, not minds."

"He just woke up. There was an argument, and he left without taking any blood."

Spencer's head spun, and his vision wavered. If

not for the women keeping him on his feet, he'd have faceplanted on the sidewalk. The scenery barely registered. He closed his eyes for a long blink, and when he opened them, Eve was guiding him into a booth in the bar.

Venus set a glass in front of him, and both women slid onto the bench across from him. "Drink," they said in unison.

Eve reached across the table to pat his hand. "The longer you avoid it, the worse you'll feel."

She was right. He was a vampire now, so he had no choice but to act like one. Picking up the glass, he brought it to his lips and instinctively inhaled. Warm, with notes of cloves and coriander, the simple scent of the blood eased the pain in his head, and the first sip was like heaven had opened shop on his tastebuds. Glorious. He tipped his head back, chugging the contents and tapping the bottom of the glass to get every last drop.

The desert in his throat turned to an oasis, and his cells hummed with energy. He set the glass down and ran a hand through his hair. "Thank you. I should have accepted the blood when Lilith offered it."

"She told us what happened," Venus said. "That must have been frightening."

"It all happened so fast, I…" He played the memory over in his mind. "Yeah, it was terrifying."

"What were you and Lilith arguing about?" Eve asked.

"My owl is dead. I know she was trying to save my life, but I'm not me without my owl. I don't know how to exist. And now I can't go out in the daylight. How will I do my job? How will I pay my bills if I can't work? I'm not…" He shook his head. It was too much to think about.

"You know you're not a normal vampire, right?" Eve frowned at her phone before slipping it into her pocket. "When Lilith turns someone, their magic is—"

"I know. The less diluted the magic, the stronger the vampire."

"And you were turned by the source, same as me," Eve said. "It will take a few days for your power to build, and your owl isn't dead. He's still inside you."

Yeah, right. "Then how do you explain the hole in my soul? When I try to call him, I can't find him."

Eve pressed her lips together and glanced at Venus. "Excuse me. I'll be right back." She rose and strode to the exit.

"You will find your owl again." Venus gave him a sympathetic look.

"What if I don't? Are we even still soulmates? My owl had claimed her, but if he's gone…" An ache spread through his chest.

"I believe you know the answer to that."

He wrung his hands on the table. He did know the answer, and he was an idiot for even posing the question. He loved Lilith with every piece of his soul that was left. If she had been the one lying on the ground, dying, and he'd had the power to save her, he'd have done it in a heartbeat.

And he'd told her he couldn't stand to look at her. "What have I done?"

"Nothing that's irreparable. You and Lilith are soulmates now and forever."

Eve approached the table, flanked by a wolf with sleek black fur and icy blue eyes. "Spencer, you know Andrei, right?"

He narrowed his eyes at the wolf. "Yeah."

Eve tapped the wolf on the shoulder before sliding into the booth. Magic shimmered around the animal, its fur dissolving as its body transformed into a man. Andrei bowed and pulled up a chair to the end of the table.

"You're a shifter?" A spark of hope ignited in his chest.

"Indeed, I am. A shifter and a vampire, as are you."

He shook his head, unable to wrap his mind around it all. "But I can't feel my owl."

Andrei chuckled. "If you had allowed her to explain rather than storming out in a huff, you would understand."

Spencer's ears burned. He'd acted like a dick.

"When Lilith turns a shifter," Andrei said, "she binds the animal until the person has control of his urges. I too believed my wolf had died when I first awoke into this life."

"Why would she do that?"

"Because the shifter she turned before me—I believe she said he was a panther—went on a murderous rampage the moment he awoke. He shifted immediately and could not contain his beast. Have your owl instincts never overridden your control?"

A tingle swept up the back of his neck to spread across his cheeks, and he lowered his gaze. There was the ferret incident… "A time or two."

Andrei nodded. "When Lilith sees that you are not in a state of bloodlust like the unfortunate soul you unearthed, she will unbind your magic and you will feel whole once more."

His stomach soured. "She did it to protect me." And he'd accused her of murder.

"Lilith would never hurt you," Eve said. "Thank you for coming so quickly, Andrei. Do you want me to walk you back to the portal?"

"Happy to be of service to you, old friend. I can find my own way." He winked at Eve before looking at Spencer. "Please, tell your friend Rebecca she is welcome in Romania any time."

As Andrei walked away, Spencer dragged his hands down his face. "Holy fuck, I screwed up. I was awful to her."

"She'll forgive you," Venus said.

"Yeah, but you've got some groveling to do." Eve crossed her arms.

"There you are!" A blonde vampire in a hot pink corset hurried toward their table. "Something's wrong with Lilith."

"She has a broken heart, but Spencer is about to mend it." Eve gave him a pointed look.

"It's worse than that. I found her in bed with Esther. The snake has turned white again, and she's as limp as a wet noodle. And Lilith is unresponsive. I think that broken heart might have killed her."

CHAPTER SEVENTEEN

Lilith wasn't dead, but she sure as hell wished she was. Esther lay lifeless beside her, and Percival sat on her pillow, his breathing quick and shallow. Deirdre had come in looking for her, but she couldn't even muster the will to acknowledge her presence. Was she being dramatic? Maybe. But what was the point of existing anymore?

She had screwed up yet again, and this time, she'd lost everything because of it. Turning Spencer was supposed to fix things. In her mind, they would be together forever, and Esther would be saved. Now, she'd lost the man she loved and her familiar. Percival wouldn't be far behind either.

What had she been thinking? Lilith, Queen of the Night, didn't deserve love. She was meant to be alone.

That fact should have been clear when she got kicked out of Eden, but no. She had refused to see it that way. She'd listened to her friends, let them convince her a soulmate existed for her, and she'd given him her whole heart. Because he *was* her soulmate. And now he was gone.

Fate was a cold-hearted bitch.

Her front door opened again, and footsteps sounded in the hall. No doubt Deirdre had called in reinforcements, but Lilith's pain couldn't be healed with a girls' night in. No amount of wine-laced blood and *Sex and the City* would make her feel better.

"Lilith?" Fear threaded through Spencer's voice, and he quickened his steps. "Oh, gods, Lilith. No."

He sank onto the bed and rested his hand on her stomach. "Esther. Percival? Oh, Lilith, I'm so sorry."

"We brought him back to you, hon." Venus's voice sounded from across the room.

Leaning down, he pressed his lips to her forehead, and a tear splashed onto her cheek as he pulled away. "I didn't mean a word of what I said. I was startled and confused, and you were right. I was so hungry I couldn't think straight."

He trailed his fingers down her cheek, and she fluttered her lids open to find him gazing at her with so much emotion in his eyes that she nearly choked on a sob. Eve and Deirdre stood next to Venus at the foot of the bed.

"Oh, thank Lucifer, you're still alive. I'm so, so sorry." Concern etched lines into Spencer's forehead, making her heart thump hard in her chest.

"*I'm* sorry," she whispered over the thickness in her throat, and her friends quietly slipped out the door, leaving them alone.

"No. You have nothing to be sorry for. You did the right thing; I can see that now. When Deirdre came into the bar and said you were dead, I…" He clamped his mouth shut, and a tear slid down his cheek. "The thought of living the rest of eternity without you was unbearable. I would have done anything to bring you back. We belong together."

She pushed to sitting and leaned her back against the headboard. "Do you really mean that?"

"I do. I saw Andrei shift. He told me how you bind a shifter's animal until he has control of his bloodlust. I should have let you explain. I should have known you wouldn't do anything to hurt me."

"Never."

"It's just… My cousin lost his owl when he was turned, so I assumed…"

She cupped his cheek in her hand. "I will release him soon."

"I love you, Lilith, with all my heart and soul." He took her hand, cradling it in both of his. "Will you be mine?"

Pressure built in the back of her eyes, and her chest gave a squeeze. "I'm a package deal, you know. If you want to have and hold me as long as we both exist, you must be willing to hold Esther and Percival too."

The crow cawed and hopped onto Spencer's leg. He laughed and stroked a finger over his feathers. "I've grown fond of this little guy."

Lilith scooped Esther into her hands. The snake wound around her wrist, responding to her touch, and her coloring turned to red, black, and yellow. "You said you hate snakes. Esther has been with me since the day I was exiled from Eden."

He eyed Esther. "I was bitten as a kid and nearly died. Am I correct in assuming I'm impervious to venom now?"

"Even if you weren't, Esther is harmless. I'm more venomous than she is." She held the snake toward him, and he nodded before reaching for her.

He let out a nervous laugh. "I'm sorry for chucking you across the room earlier. I didn't know who you were." He held her loosely, and she flicked out her tongue, slithering up his arm and around the back of his shoulders.

Lilith's smile widened, and her heart felt like a rabbit's foot thumping against her breastbone. "She likes you."

"I like her too. She's part of you." Esther spiraled her way down his other arm, returning to Lilith.

"Well, then." She rose from the bed and placed her beneath the heat lamp. Closing her eyes, she reached out to connect with her familiar, and the bond formed immediately as if poor Esther hadn't resided on Azrael's doorstep for the past month. All was well.

"In answer to your question, yes." She sank onto the bed next to him. "I will be yours. I have been since the moment we met, and I will be for as long as you'll have me."

"As long as I don't get staked or beheaded, how does eternity sound?"

She smiled as a thousand butterflies flitted from her stomach to her chest. "Better than heaven."

He took her cheek in his hand and placed a tender kiss on her lips. Heat unfurled in her belly, and she leaned into him, gripping his thigh and slipping her tongue into his mouth. His new fangs grazed her flesh, the razor-like tips drawing blood. A moan rumbled in his chest, and she pulled back to gaze into his eyes.

"Be careful of your fangs. They're sharp."

He slipped out his tongue to moisten his lips. "You taste amazing."

"Play your cards right, and I might let you have more."

"Vampires can drink each other's blood?"

"Not for sustenance, but for intimacy."

He parted his lips, touching the tip of his tongue to his fang. Lilith's gaze locked on his mouth, and the heat in her belly rolled down to her nether region. Her soulmate was now a vampire. Sure, the circumstances surrounding his transformation weren't as either of them would have liked, but Spencer was immortal now. He was hers forever, and the mere thought made tears gather on her lower lids.

"Then let's get intimate." Fire sparked in his eyes, and he took her mouth in another kiss, this one filled with urgency and passion.

Percival cawed and flew out of the room, and she grabbed Spencer's shirt, tugging it upward, only breaking the kiss to yank it over his head. Their mouths met again, and she wrapped her arms around him, massaging the bare skin on his back as they kissed. He broke away, rising to his feet and pulling her up with him.

He took off her shirt and bra and pulled her to his chest. His skin was cooler than before, but he was a vampire now, so that was normal. He was still soft and hard in all the right places, and she unbuttoned his pants to reach for her favorite hard thing. She wrapped her fingers around his dick, and he sucked in a breath.

"All of my senses are ten times stronger." He undid her pants and worked them down her hips, taking her panties with them.

"What I'm about to do to you will feel ten times better." She pushed his pants down and started to lower to her knees.

"Mm-mm." He clutched her shoulders, stopping her descent. "Let me worship you."

Before she could respond, he scooped an arm behind her knees, lifting her from her feet and placing her on the bed. Her stomach fluttered, and a warm shiver ran down her spine. If he wanted to worship her, who was she to deny him?

He kicked off his pants and tossed the rest of their clothes aside before climbing on top of her. He kissed her neck, running his tongue up to her ear before gliding his nose down to her shoulder with a deep inhale. "I can smell your blood. The urge to taste it is overwhelming."

"The wait will be worth it."

"I know." Rising to his hands and knees, he held her gaze and moved back. He pressed a kiss to her navel before spreading her legs and lying between them. "I want to taste the rest of you first."

He flicked out his tongue, bathing her clit, and electricity shot straight to her heart. An *ahh* escaped her lips, and she arched her back, offering her whole self to him. He licked her again, and she moaned.

"I love the sounds you make." His words vibrated through her core.

"I love it when you make me make them." She fisted the sheets as he worked his tongue, pleasuring her and moaning his appreciation. Every nerve in her body felt alive in a way she'd never experienced before. Sparkling with energy and magic and love.

He slipped two fingers inside her, angling his hand to reach her sweet spot and stroking the sensitive flesh until she cried out his name. Her climax tightened in her core, begging to be released. She was almost there.

"Bite me, Spencer. On my inner thigh."

He inhaled deeply, pressing his thumb against her clit and gliding his lips across to her leg. "Here?"

he whispered against her skin, turning it to gooseflesh.

"Yes. Sweet Persephone, please."

He sank his fangs into her thigh, and a million fireworks exploded inside her, the orgasm rocking her soul. A groan vibrated from his lips as he covered the puncture with his mouth and sucked. Wave after wave of ecstasy washed over her until she couldn't bear the pleasure anymore.

Panting, she stilled his hand, and he released her, gazing up with passion-drunk eyes.

"My turn." She pushed to sitting. "On your back."

He rose to his knees, gripping his cock, and moisture beaded on his tip. "I need to be inside you. Right now."

With a wicked grin, she pushed him down and straddled him, sinking onto his dick and gasping as he filled her. Still incredibly sensitive from her orgasm, she moved slowly, rising up and sliding down, reveling in the pleasant ache of his girth.

He held her hips and ran his hands over her body, caressing her skin. "I love you."

His words washed over her, wrapping around her like a blanket, hugging her tight. "I love you too."

She leaned down for a kiss and increased her

rhythm, going faster, harder. He groaned and gripped her thighs, encouraging her to continue her speed. They fit together perfectly, and he thrust his hips beneath her, matching her rhythm beat for beat until another orgasm spiraled in her core.

"Are you ready?" she asked.

"Gods, yes." He leaned his head to the side, giving her access to his neck.

She bit, and as his blood bathed her tongue, she came. Her entire body shuddered with her release, and she stilled, giving Spencer full control.

He thrust harder, harder, faster, faster, his fingers digging into her flesh before he slammed into her, grinding his pelvis into hers as he found his release.

His grip loosened, and she lay on top of him, covering his body with hers, unwilling to end the intimacy just yet. It had taken millennia, but the world's first woman had finally found her match. Fate had given her another chance at love, and this time, she was taking it.

Lilith donned the magical clothing Arachne had made for her and paced down the street toward the network offices. It was midday, and the dastardly sun beat down on her shoulders. Thankfully, the SPF one thousand did its job, and she only felt a tingle of fatigue. Nothing she couldn't handle.

Sadly, Percival and Esther had to stay home for this adventure. Humans didn't take kindly to a woman walking into a professional building with a snake draped over her shoulders. Go figure.

Frigid air engulfed her as she stepped inside the high rise, and she removed her hat, folding it and tucking it into a magical pocket. She slipped her sunglasses into the other one and boarded the elevator to head to the fourteenth floor.

Spencer said she needed to sign a release and attend a meeting before the Romania episode could air. Why she had to venture out to do this when electronic signatures and video calls existed, she wasn't sure. But Spencer insisted, and she would move The Underworld and Earth for the man she loved.

She smiled at the thought of him. He'd gotten control of his bloodlust quickly, and the light in his eyes when she'd released his owl, making him whole, would forever be her favorite memory.

The elevator door slid open, revealing Spencer, Alan, and Rebecca sitting on a bench in the lobby. He shot to his feet and strode toward her, taking her shoulders in his hands and kissing her cheek. "Thanks for coming."

"Of course. I like your outfit." She winked.

Spencer wore a custom-tailored suit, SPF one thousand. His light brown hair was freshly trimmed —the last haircut he would ever need—and his deep brown eyes sparkled with excitement. "The execs loved the Romania episode."

"You saved our show." Alan rose and strode toward them, followed by Rebecca.

"We can't thank you enough," she said.

Lilith's smile widened. "The pleasure was mine,

really. I'm happy to help on any future episodes as well. I do have connections."

"That's why I asked you to come." Spencer glanced at his friends, and they nodded. "Mary, the head of programming, is interested in the redhead who shined on camera."

A giggle rose from her chest. "I don't know about shined."

"When she asked who you were…" Spencer lowered his gaze, biting his lip before looking into her eyes. "I told her you were our new head of research."

She blinked. "What…?"

"She wants to hire you. She…we…want you to be part of our team."

Her lips parted on a gasp. "So I would go on all of your adventures?"

"And help us plan them." He took her hand. "What do you say? Join our team? Be our partner?"

They were at his place of employment, and she needed to act professionally, but at that moment, she didn't care. She threw her arms around him and planted a kiss on his lips. "Do you even have to ask? Of course I'll join you."

She rested her head on his shoulder, and a tear slid down her cheek. Never, in thousands of years, would she ever have believed she could love someone this much. She had found a partner in life and now a purpose…all thanks to speed dating.

A woman in a pencil skirt and a blue silk blouse stepped toward them. "*The Hunt for Cryptids?*"

"That's us." Spencer released Lilith and smoothed his suit.

"Mary will see you now." She gestured toward an open door.

Spencer beamed. "Ready to start your career?"

She straightened her spine, her smile making her cheeks ache, and she nodded. "Indeed, I am."

New Orleans Nocturnes Series

License to Bite

Shift Happens

Life's a Witch

Santa Got Run Over by a Vampire

Finders Reapers

Swipe Right to Bite

Batshift Crazy

Holy Shift

Collection One: Books 1-3

Collection Two: Books 4-7

Crescent City Wolf Pack Series

Werewolves Only

Beneath a Blue Moon

Bound by Blood

A Deal with Death

A Song to Remember

Shifting Fate

Collection One: Books 1-3

Collection Two: Books 4-6

Haunted Ever After Series

Love at First Haunt

Second Chance Spirit

Third Time's a Ghost

Love and Ghosts

Love and Omens

Love and Curses

Collection One: Books 1 - 3

Collection Two: Books 4 - 6

Lessons in Divine Disasters Series

How to Steal a God's Heart

How to Flirt With the Angel of Death

How to Woo the World's First Vampire

Stand Alone Books

Flipping the Bird

The Rest of Forever

Soul Catchers

Bewitching the Vampire

ABOUT THE AUTHOR

Carrie Pulkinen is a paranormal romance author who has always been fascinated with things that go bump in the night. Of course, when you grow up next door to a cemetery, the dead (and the undead) are hard to ignore. Pair that with her passion for writing and her love of a good happily-ever-after, and becoming a paranormal romance author seems like the only logical career choice.

Before she decided to turn her love of the written word into a career, Carrie spent the first part of her professional life as a high school journalism and yearbook teacher. She loves good chocolate and bad puns, and in her free time, she likes to dance, drink wine, and travel with her family.

Connect with Carrie online:
CarriePulkinen.com